LAND BEYOND THE SEA

By KEVIN MAJOR

Fiction

Hold Fast
Far From Shore
Thirty-Six Exposures
Dear Bruce Springsteen
Blood Red Ochre
Eating Between the Lines
Diana: My Autobiography
No Man's Land
Gaffer
Ann and Seamus
One for the Rock

The Newfoundland trilogy:
New Under the Sun
Found Far and Wide
Land Beyond the Sea

Non-Fiction

Free the Children (with Craig Kielburger)
As Near to Heaven by Sea: A History of Newfoundland and Labrador
Printmaking on the Edge: 40 Years at St. Michael's

Drama

No Man's Land: A Play
Lead Me Home

Children

The House of Wooden Santas
Eh? To Zed: A Canadian ABeCedarium
Aunt Olga's Christmas Postcards

LAND BEYOND THE SEA

KEVIN MAJOR

Breakwater Books
P.O. Box 2188, St. John's, NL, Canada, A1C 6E6
www.breakwaterbooks.com

ISBN 978-1-55081-752-2

Author photo: Victoria Wells
Cover photo: Shutterstock

A CIP catalogue record for this book is available from Library and Archives Canada.

We acknowledge the support of the Canada Council for the Arts, which last year invested $153 million to bring the arts to Canadians throughout the country. We acknowledge the financial support of the Government of Canada and the Government of Newfoundland and Labrador through the Department of Tourism, Culture, Industry and Innovation for our publishing activities.

Printed and bound in Canada.

Breakwater Books is committed to choosing papers and materials for our books that help to protect our environment. To this end, this book is printed on a recycled paper and other controlled sources that is certified by the Forest Stewardship Council®.

Canada Council for the Arts   Conseil des Arts du Canada

For Minette, in whose home I first heard the story of the Caribou,
and in memory of Roland Major and Mark Genge

THAT UNGODLY SLICE OF TIME, THAT VISCERAL JERK OF the lever. That thrust of metal and clamp of magnet. That thunderstroke of torpedo, 200 kilograms of hexanite erupting into hellfire.

That voltage surge through every limb. Apex of our incessant training, so fixed in the heads of U-boatmen that once in motion there is no stop to it.

14 October 1942.
0534 Wind light from the west, sea state—calm, cloud cover—0.1, barometer—1026 mb, very good visibility, faint northern lights.

Recorded at first sighting. 0534 German Legal Time. Off Newfoundland, still more than six hours to sunrise. This, in my own hand, the war diary of U-boat 69.

One shadow in sight, behind it a second smaller one. Enemy course 40°, speed 10.5 knots. Strongly smoking freight passenger steamer.

On return to base at Lorient a typed copy of this log, my name, Ulrich Gräf, signed at the end of each day, made its way to Admiral Dönitz at U-boat headquarters in Paris.

To this log of eighty-three days, Dönitz appended his comment.

The commander was always tough and ready to try for success.

Of course I was hoping for more. The comment did draw attention to itself on the page. It left me satisfied, within reason. Dönitz is never effusive. I had demonstrated I am capable of more.

Indeed, Admiral Dönitz, this is true.

OCTOBER 1942

THERE HAS BEEN NOTHING BEYOND THE IRON Cross. Nothing new to chafe the throat.

20,000 GRT. Six ships sunk. No matter. I did not join the *Kriegsmarine* for future glory.

It was glory enough to be chosen. This we knew from the outset, from the minute we set foot in our *Gymnasium* as schoolboys. For every sturdy scamp to cross that threshold, another nine had been abandoned to schools of lesser rank. When we finally disembarked at Dänholm to start our training, expectations ran high.

There is a photograph of a squad of us nineteen year olds—shirtless, sweat-soaked, arms slung about each other's shoulders—a squad of that dauntless crew of 1935, our smiles decisively set despite a day of barbaric drills and ruthless hounding at the hands of *Korporal* Jodeit.

No officer forgets his *Korporal,* a tyrant he'll outrank in short order.

I had already received a steady dose of his caustic tongue when, on the third day in barracks, he caught sight of my sketchbook. I had carelessly left the edge of it exposed. He slipped it from beneath the blanket, settled himself on a corner of the bed, leafed through it page by page.

'An artist, Seaman Gräf? A master of the pencil sketch?'

'An interest only, *Korporalschaftsführer*.'

He took me to be taunting him. 'You are too modest, Seaman Gräf.' He tore a page from the book, a sketch of a bend in the river Elbe, one of my best, not yet finished. 'I shall like this for my room. I am fond of waterways. A bit wild to my taste, but I will overlook the impatience in the stroke. Your stroke is always impatient, I suspect, no matter what you have in your hand.'

I showed no sign of disrespect. I smiled. He carefully closed the book and slipped it back beneath the blanket.

'Our secret, Seaman Gräf. Each time you raise your pencil think of this sketch pinned above my bed. It will make you the better artist, will it not?' He grinned.

'*Jawohl, Korporalschaftsführer*.'

Before he left our barracks room, each man poker-stiff, right hand in rigid salute, Jodeit waved the page from the sketchbook above his head. 'Gentlemen, you have an artist among you! A fledgling Friedrich! Perhaps he does portraits, gentlemen. Perhaps he will want you to bare your bodies for his sketchbook. Beware, he may have his eye on you.'

He turned and was gone and I was left with a roomful of ribald comrades mocking me like hell.

Their laughter eventually died away. Each of us had his own justification for despising Jodeit, many more lacerating than my own. I was of reasonable height and in prime physical shape, but for those who were not, *Herr Korporal* had a particular storehouse of abuse. A few he had made to suffer horribly, though he failed to break us. Together we chiselled an iron will, even as we lay bone-weary and ragged in the few minutes before sleep each night. A fellow hiding a sketchbook was of little consequence.

The sketchbook was my lifeline in Dänholm, despite the fact I did not add much to it while there. No time, though there were moments slogging through sand dunes, machine gun like concrete in my hands, when the sketches of Otto Dix flooded my mind.

Dix's grotesques of war would never do a man in basic training. In any event he was banned by then from the public eye, an artist labelled "degenerate" by the Reich. Two years before, I had seen paintings of his on the walls of the *Neues Rathaus* in Dresden, Dix and dozens more, including my former teacher Herr Lachnit. The Lord Mayor paraded about in his party uniform, the official arbitrator of artistic merit.

Dix I could put out of my mind. Not so another on those same walls, Franz Marc. At times I lived for the wild vigour of his animals, the brilliance of his colours. "Blue is the male principle," he wrote, "astringent and spiritual." Navy blue, I like to think.

What then was I doing in military service to my country when my heart was with the Academy? One measure of that heart only, and no longer the foremost. For other measures took its place. The physical, the rivalry of classmates, the prowess of the *Kriegsmarine* all proved stronger incentives.

A man is a man of many virtues.

She's been called many things, but mostly Bride. She has never been one, and now at sixty-one, it is not likely she ever will. Still, the woman has no regrets. From what Bride knows of men, she looks back on her life and thinks herself the one blessed.

There was Gerald, and they had their time, and a good time it was, too. Gerald had his laudable points, and there are nights she still longs for the heft of his nakedness, followed by the laughter that curled around the breakfast table. But in the end it didn't work out, as they say.

Now she has the good fortune of meeting the man of her lost dreams ten times a day, every day she's aboard—Canadians, Americans, Brits, Newfoundlanders—trim and uniformed and full of charms she hardly wants to imagine. Some so young and wanton it makes the gap between the years an abyss. But better this than nothing at all, she long ago concluded. It keeps her mind active. It does that to be sure.

Miss Fitzpatrick, he calls her.

The young man is in desperate need of something she's not been able to put her finger on, not exactly. The uniform he's wearing is that of a ship steward. Unfortunately, it won't get him very far with any of the young ladies aboard the *Caribou*.

She calls him Johnny. He'd prefer John.

John is his own man. Bride saw it the first time she laid eyes on him, years ago now, the fellow hell-bent on making his way from Newfoundland to New York. When the other passengers had settled down for the night she pulled him aside in the lounge, sat him down, and told him about New York. She'd had a stretch of ten years in Manhattan.

The young man's stepfather had left Newfoundland to work high steel and helped build the Empire State, according to John. So New York wasn't as foreign to him as she had imagined. Still for all, he was in for a few things that would set him on his ear. That was certain.

Then, eight months later, there was John Gilbert again, finished up in New York and on his way back home to St. Anthony. And, hardly a surprise to her, the next year Bride received a letter, wondering if there might be a job for him aboard the *Caribou*. John was out-and-out restless. He still is.

He waits patiently until he has her attention. 'The Stricklands are wanting a larger cabin. There's four of them and only two single bunks.'

'There are no more cabins.'

Bride stands there until she sees John turn and head down the stairwell. She's thinking there's a chance he might make chief steward someday. The potential is there, she's concluded, once he settles down and gets a few more years under his belt. He's not good at taking orders from a woman, which makes him no different than most of them, but then Bride never expects otherwise. It'll take time, but they all learn to live with it. They have no choice.

It was the same in Manhattan. The young bucks would look at her and smile, figuring they could do a better job. That didn't last. It was either smarten up or go back to tramping the sidewalks. She didn't get her position at the Waldorf on the off chance it might work out. She knew what needed to be done, saw it was done, and kept the guests smiling.

Why then did she leave it all after ten years? She'd walk the streets of the city on her way to work, walk by the Empire State and think to herself, they won't be seeing one like that in Newfoundland very quick. She'd look up, focus on the very tip of its spire then look around her at the flurry of people about the sidewalks. She'd stand there and wonder—what holds anyone to one spot?

Family? Not Bride. Excitement? There was no shortage of that in New York City. But after a time it wore thin. She longed for that connection to home. And that's what Bride enjoys aboard the *Caribou*. Every time the ferry leaves Nova Scotia she's heading home again. And what's more exciting than a crowd of soldiers and sailors singing and dancing around a piano? Airmen, that's what.

A mariner who smokes a pipe does well to do it on deck. Even in winter. Though it's not quite winter yet. It's an October night on the dull black deck of the ship he has captained for fourteen years.

The deck is faintly burnished by the moon. Ben Taverner has one hand clamped against the enameled iron railing, drawing on his well-aged briar in an erratic rhythm calculated not to show any spark. He has constantly drawn from it peace of mind, but tonight the tobacco has gone dead and no amount of effort renews it.

A disembodied voice. 'Captain. Sir.'

There is a tautness to the words that irks Taverner, though he'd never raise it to this third officer, his son.

Taverner answers with the officer's proper name. 'Harold.'

With each step, Harold reveals more of himself, emerging from the black of night, his cap-shrouded features last of all. There is containment in the look he gives his father, in the portion his father can detect even face-to-face, that deepens the unease. For the moment he looks older, older than Stanley, the other son aboard. Harold is twenty-four.

Taverner doubts his son would want to know what's on his mind. Regardless, he tells him.

'The *Caribou* is no more than an unrepentant thief in the night.'

'The Germans sank the *Waterton* and not a man was lost. The *Vision* rescued them all.'

Harold is right. But that was thanks to the mercy of daylight. Had it been dark, it would have been another story.

The captain is rarely fired, even to this point. Only those closest to him ever witness an emotional response. For most of the crew he is autonomous, single-minded. They expect nothing less than unreserved calm.

Harold has seen it falter. He has learned to predict it. And to some measure, welcome it.

For several months now Ben Taverner has been at odds to understand his son, why he's eager to stand up for the Canadians. They were caught by surprise, as Harold would have it. And they are doing all they can, under the circumstances.

Including, it goes without saying, ignoring warnings from the man who knows the Cabot Strait better than anyone alive.

The *S.S. Caribou* is a civilian vessel.

But more than half of Taverner's 191 passengers are military, on their way back to their bases in Newfoundland. And not for a second does Taverner believe German intelligence isn't aware of that.

Harold insists the Jerries have more than the *Caribou* on their minds.

Taverner looks at his son and sees stubborn inexperience. There's no talking sense to him.

For several months Harold was a merchant seaman on the Great Lakes, working alongside the Canadians. It's not what he wants now, to be aboard the *Caribou*. Why, Taverner wonders. Why wouldn't someone want to work his way up to captain when the opportunity is presented to him on a silver platter?

Stanley would be happy enough to take over when his father retires. He likely expects it. Yet it's Harold who has the intellect, the natural instinct for the sea. Enough, Taverner had told him straight out, to be in charge of any ship afloat.

Another Taverner captain.

Why wouldn't a son be proud of that?

The ship pushes on, phantom in the dead of night, belching black, coal-driven smoke. There are no blackout curtains for the moon.

Every scrap of me strove for the day the field-grey uniforms were cast aside and we donned Navy blues, ours to traipse about on day leave as we pleased. The girls of Stralsund slithered about their doorways and smiled. Our first taste of the lure of the uniform.

The three months that followed we spent in the Baltic aboard the *Gorch Fock*, the navy's square-rigged barque that on the right day could show two thousand square meters of sail. A magnificent vessel, if one as far removed from a U-boat as possible.

Ah, but we were not U-boat men yet. We were lusty cadets, desperate to demonstrate our seamanship. Desperate to climb the ratlines and man the yards, in breakneck compliance with the bellow from the lungs of our *Oberbootsmann* Kühn. We were lowly seamen at the mercy of heartless corporals, anxious to see us squirm in their filth.

Doomed was the man assigned for the day to the corporals' quarters. 'You think yourself too good for this clean-up, Gräf?' Their quarters reeked of armpit sweat and beer and stale cigarette smoke. *Jan Maat* without doubt. My friends and I smoked better brands.

A corporal dropped out of his hammock, creased and twisted in his underwear, flatulence ripping from him as he landed next to me. 'We are under the impression you cadets like the smell of shit.'

I said nothing and allowed the laughter to run its course.

We had not a doubt we would survive them. Some nights a small batch of us stowed ourselves in the obscurity of the safety net under the jib boom. It was there I got to know Teddy Suhren, future ace, future pet of the Reich. Based on what I saw of him then, I would hardly credit his recent turn of good fortune. He had his savage barbs for the corporals, as did we all. But Suhren was a daredevil, more than most, and perhaps that was it. The Party found something to like in a clever daredevil, one with luck on his side.

Suhren had his imaginative twist on survival, which appealed to me. The bow of the ship cut through the phosphorescence of the open seas and in the darkness we were eager young mortals of any century, relishing the raw gifts of nature.

We could be silent then and hold to that moment. When the silence was broken, it was Suhren groaning out the words of Gorch Fock, the poet turned sailor from Hamburg , whose name emblazoned our ship.

Dicke Berta heet ik,
Tweeunveertig meet ik!
Wat ik kann, dat week ik!
Söben Milen scheet ik...

The rest of us joined in. We all knew the riotous words about Big Bertha, our massive howitzer. Our rumbling voices sounded like an underwater chorus, our laughter barely muffled at the end.

Fock would not have known this grand windjammer was named after him. He was killed in the Battle of Jutland in 1916. We visited his gravesite during this voyage of his namesake.

If I sound a note of skepticism, let's be clear—there is no room for such a trait in the *Kriegsmarine*. My U-boatmen have utter faith in me. Their lives are in my hands. To be more precise, in my hands and those of the men who transmit the orders. There is an iron chain of hands and at the end an iron wall of command.

We captains are very fond of our Admiral Dönitz. U-boatmen are his personal force and he has their unqualified respect. *Der Löwe* was there to greet U-69 and her bearded, sunburnt crew on the 25th of June when she slipped back into Saint-Nazaire from the West Indies, at the end of my first patrol as her commander. Four ships had been sunk, none of any great tonnage, 12,000 GRT the total. But enough that I proved my worth. The admiral had greater things in mind for my second time out, as did I.

When he stepped on deck and shook my hand he immediately put me at ease. He has that way. I have known him to take money from his own pocket and slip it to a commander running short and in need of a good time in Paris before his next patrol.

'A promising start, *Oberleutnant* Gräf. The Caribbean agreed with you.'

'Yes, sir,' I said, smiling. 'Hot as hell, sir.' The time on deck had been pleasant enough, but the long dives were diesel-reeking steam baths, water dripping from every metal surface. At times the men could barely breathe.

Our prize had been the *Lise*, a Norwegian oil tanker in the service of the Tommies. We struck her not far off Curaçao, first by torpedo, then shelling to her gun platform. I ordered a halt and gave those who were left alive their allotted time to abandon ship, before the master stroke that sent her to the bottom.

Our enemy is the ship, not her men. We allow them their survival where we can. The Tommies would have us with horns protruding from our heads. Such is war. Truth wavers between enemies. The crew of the schooner *James E. Newsom* would know the truth, chewing the rations we dropped into their lifeboat.

I leave no doubt—our priority is the safety of the U-boat. It would be lunacy otherwise, to put my men in harm's way for the sake of survivors. But if there is the scope to give aid to those left in the wake of a sinking, then we do what we can to give them a decent chance. Other captains have done the same. To the surprise of the survivors it goes without saying.

The Führer would fume at the notion. Yet the navy never revels in the sight of drowning men. It is not in our code of conduct.

BRIDE COUNTS HERSELF A FORTUNATE ONE. SHE'S LANDED in the middle of a turnaround in Newfoundland.

When she left for the United States the island's economy was in shambles. There was hardly a job to be had. A country practically bankrupt, so far in debt the government went to Britain for a bailout. The British held up a fistful of cheques with one hand and with the other shook on a deal that forced Newfoundland to relinquish self-government. It was a hefty price to pay, to Bride's mind. Was there ever another country that fought for the right to govern itself, only to give it all up with a smile and a handshake?

Newfoundland is back in the hands of the British. In any case, it has never had any flag except the Union Jack. Commission of Government it is called, a commission of three representatives from Britain and three from Newfoundland, set up to administer the country. There's plenty who argue it's the reason the island is better off. Bride is not one of them. At least, they say, there's not a House of Assembly in St. John's living the life of Riley, while the poor devils in the outports are half-starved to death. That much Bride concedes. She saw families go desperately hungry when she was growing up, more than she cares to remember.

But, and this she knows for a fact, it's not Britain who saved the day, it's Uncle Sam. It's the war. The United States set its eyes on that bit of North America closest to the war, and then came knocking, handed over to the British fifty destroyers in return for the right to establish military bases in Newfoundland, and in Labrador. The Americans brought their stacks of money and their G.I.s by the thousands.

Like the fellow standing in front of her. White teeth, chewing gum, Vitalis. He's heading back to his base, as are the rest of them.

Ma'am, he calls her. And he's come all the way from Texas. His name is Hank.

'And Pennsylvania, ma'am.'

They always have a buddy. If not before they board the ship, then five minutes after. They've been on leave, both of them. Back home to see their families.

'And to pick up a few new tunes,' according to Buzz.

Buzz loves a piano. 'Happier than a coonhound on a bare leg,' as Hank would have it. Bride shakes her head and smiles. It could be her entertainment for the whole evening.

The pair are sharing a cabin. But Hank, Bride suspects, would be more than willing to trade in his piano-playing friend should a promising young lady come along.

He holds out a stick of Juicy Fruit and the gleam of his pearly whites. Bride shakes her head with a slight twist of her lips. Hank slips the gum away without a second thought.

When Buzz seats himself at the piano it's like a hand slinking into a glove. He starts to play, without the least of preliminaries.

Hank recognizes the tune. He grins broadly. If he's to be believed he was singing that very song not two days ago, to some girl on a platform in Grand Central Station.

Hank is all Yank, and a charmer to the core. He can sweet talk his way past a girl's good sense in the blink of an eye. He lives his life as if tomorrow is a million miles away. But what he wakes up to the next morning is the long arm of war, and now that the Americans are in it, he could be shipped to Europe before that grin ever gets the chance to wear off.

Buzz is having his go at "When the Lights Go On Again." Hank picks up the first line, and for the moment Bride's caution melts away. Soon they are harmonizing as if there's no war, only the songs that go with it. Bride leans into the piano and, had she a mother's heart to give them, they would have it all.

She ends her singing as quickly as it began. She lets the business of the boat drag her away. Some nights she's pulled six ways from Sunday.

William Lundrigan has drifted into the lounge. He's wearing an olive-green trench coat, belted over a suit and tie. He sets down a leather suitcase, well-made and well-worn, neatly strapped. William Lundrigan is a building contractor and one of the island's leading businessmen. He's done very well by the arrival of the American military in Newfoundland.

Bride had noticed his name on the purser's passenger list. She discreetly inquires about his trip to Montreal. Lundrigan had been on the ship the week before, en route to the mainland for medical treatment.

He assures her that everything went well. She's not sure exactly what the concern was. She suspects it was his heart. She's not about to ask, but he does look like all his travelling has taken its toll. He's anxious to get settled into his cabin for the night.

Bride glances about for a steward to take Lundrigan's suitcase down to his room. He agrees it would be a help. He's not supposed to be lifting.

Hernia, Bride thinks now. She leans into the hallway and calls for John.

Before he shows up, there arrives a woman, a Mrs. Shiers, as Bride recalls from the purser's list.

The woman has a crying baby in her arms. She's looking for someone in charge. She makes for Bride, distraught. She has no cabin, no place to settle her child, and insists they can't be sitting up the whole night.

Bride's sympathy is guarded. The woman would have had a cabin had she thought ahead and made the arrangements. Bride tells her it's the purser she should be talking to.

She's done that. The military gets first chance at any cabins that haven't been pre-arranged, and the fact that her husband is in the Canadian Navy has no bearing on the situation. The child, Leonard, needs his sleep and she's willing to share a cabin.

Bride peers over at Hank. Is the American military willing to share? She's heartened to see the G.I. squirm.

Lundrigan steps in. He offers his cabin to the woman. He has children of his own. Twelve in fact. The youngest no older than Mrs. Shiers's little one. Lundrigan tells Bride to fix it up with the purser.

That's something she is not about to do. She pointedly informs Mrs. Shiers that Lundrigan is not a well man, that he has just undergone an operation and needs his proper rest.

Nonsense, he tells Bride. Lundrigan retrieves the room key from his pocket and places it in the hand of Mrs. Shiers.

It's not Bride's place to argue with him, as much as it is in her to do exactly that.

Where will he lie down? On the divan in the lounge is the only answer, to her mind no better than if he had walked aboard the boat off skid row, not a dime to his name. Bride is left without a word.

Some would say a captain is only as good as his crew. As Taverner sees it, a captain gets the best out of the crew because he expects the best. He runs a ship every one of them can be proud of, but that happens because he makes sure it happens. He doesn't lack for confidence.

Taverner often dwells on the other pairs of brothers aboard, besides his own two sons. To him it says a lot.

Among them the Hanns—Harry and Clarence. The Gales—George and Jerome. The Coffins—Elijah and Bert. Six pairs in all and to a man eager to sign on, despite what their wives and mothers might have said. His men know the dangers as well as he does. He admires the way they brush them off, their cockiness.

There's a distraction, the noise of someone approaching. A man emerges from the dark, hat drawn firm, his woolen trench coat tightly belted, its collar up.

It's Lundrigan. Taverner knew he was aboard, but is surprised he hasn't settled into his cabin long ago. He warns him to be careful not to catch cold.

Lundrigan came from very little. His first job paid him fifty cents a day. At fifteen he quit school to help support the family after his father was disabled in a mining accident. He worked as a miner, a travelling salesman, the owner of a small grocery store. Then came his logging and lumbering operations. Now he has a dozen irons in the fire and works dog hard to make the most of them. A man forever pushing ahead.

The men have pronounced respect for each other. The captain holds out his hand. Lundrigan shakes it, although not as vigorously as the last time he was aboard.

'Just in need of a little air,' he tells Taverner.

Lundrigan knows Stanley from his previous trips but he has not met Harold. He extends his hand. 'Rare must be a captain who shares the operation of his vessel with two of his progeny.' The handshake leads him to something he has often considered. 'The love for the sea, is it in the blood?'

'Yes, in the blood.' Taverner has no doubt. Trinity, where Taverner grew up, had fishing ships in its harbour since the 1500s. Portuguese, English, French. The place was alive with schooners when he was a boy. As soon as he was old enough to quit school, he was gone from Newfoundland, aboard the first vessel that would take him on. Ben Taverner had his British Foreign Going Masters Certificate by the time he was twenty. 'I was going to have a life on the water, never a second thought.'

'Driven,' Lundrigan suggests. It takes a driven man to get things done. And a stubborn one.

Taverner could have worked out of any port in the empire, if he'd had the mind for it. For a Newfoundlander there is always that tug back to the island, back home, no matter how long he's been away. A weakness some would say, but it's more than the familiar, more than circumstance.

Newfoundland, as Taverner sees it, is in desperate need of strong men to set it right. How good it is to see Lundrigan putting his fellow Newfoundlanders to work, allowing men to draw a decent wage. How good it is to see someone put a stop to the drain of men to the United States and Canada.

'And just where does Harold fit into all this?'

'I just came off the Great Lakes,' Harold admits. 'I could have stayed there if I wanted. I decided to come back home.'

Lundrigan peers at him. 'Even if it's not a very safe one at the moment?'

The captain is taken aback. He had thought every passenger had full trust in crossing the Strait.

Lundrigan concedes he had considered taking a TCA flight to Gander.

But he didn't.

Harold is more definite. 'It's the Cabot Strait, not the Strait of Gibraltar, sir.'

Harold has chosen to say nothing about the *Waterton*. Neither does his father. Or nothing about the U-boat attack the month before on the ore carriers anchored off Bell Island. Twenty-nine men lost. There is no point in making Lundrigan more anxious than he is already.

Every passenger knows his lifeboat station. And the Canadian Navy has provided the *Caribou* with a dozen Carley life rafts.

The man was on his way to check out his station. Taverner nods. There is no harm in being sure of the route.

'We're safe enough then. Good evening to you both, gentlemen.' They extend to him the same and watch as he disappears.

It could be said the Germans have made him a rich man, Harold notes, if anyone is willing to look at it that way.

HIS JOKE RAN THROUGH THE *U-BOOTWAFFE* LIKE WILDFIRE. Suhren arrived in Brest after his last patrol, another 32,000 GRT under his belt. Picture it. He called through the megaphone to his friend, Hein Uphoff, who had tied up his own U-boat just ahead of him. 'Hein,' he called, 'are the Nazis still at the helm then?'

Only Teddy Suhren could get away with such an insult. On the pier to greet him was the chief of the flotilla. No doubt the Knight's Cross with Oak Leaves and Crossed Swords hanging below Suhren's chin was enough reason for the chief to stiffen, wordless, as if he had heard nothing.

There is no doubting our loyalty. On Dänholm we were four hundred sinewy cadets, our right arms erect, our voices thundering in unison, as if the Führer himself were standing before us on the parade square. 'I swear by God this holy oath, that I will render to Adolf Hitler, Führer of the German Reich and People, Supreme Commander of the Armed Forces, unconditional obedience, and that I am ready, as a brave soldier, to risk my life at any time for this oath.'

Words a man does not deliver lightly.

The Führer returned our pride in the Homeland, after the Treaty of Versailles ripped it away. The Poles got what they deserved. They had no right to our land. I know too well my father's stories of families forced from their farms by insolent

Poles. Father has no more liking for the arrogant French, who demanded we bear all guilt for the First War, as if our millions killed were not suffering enough. The French would have us boot-lick forevermore.

I was torpedo officer at the training school in Flensburg-Mürwik in November of 1938. We knew nothing of *die Kristallnacht*.

I had boyhood friends who were Jews. I went home on leave and saw their synagogue had been burned and the ruins carted off, that edifice built by Semper, the same man who built our Opera House. Father, who took great pride in the architecture of his city, told me the Brownshirts were behind it. Not only them, said my mother. Hundreds of Jews had their jobs taken away, and my friend, Josef, among them. Josef's mother says Jews have been cut to the bone by the regulations.

'I have not seen Josef for years. We have no choice but put it out of our minds,' Father said. 'They bring it on themselves. The Jews and their money.'

'Shame on you, Walter. Shame!'

It was the cause of great grief between my parents, and I escaped back to the *Marineschule*, far away from politics.

No one said we were preparing for war, but we would be prepared if it came. The Führer returned to the Imperial Navy the glory it had once known, nothing less. The country would go about its business and the navy would grow steadily stronger, led by men of the highest rank. All a matter of pride, something we Germans had been told we should never have again. It is laughable to think a country could exist without pride in itself, as if we were some corner of Africa or Asia.

Once we ended our training aboard the *Gorch Fock*, we spent nine months touring the world. Nothing did us more good than setting ourselves against foreign soil. We stood honoured at being German, for in no place did we find the will to excel, such as we had known since we were schoolboys. What good is freedom if not bolstered by ambition?

Half our number went aboard the cruiser *Emden*. The other half, myself included, set sail from Kiel aboard the *Karlsruhe*. We stopped in places as far flung as Batavia and Hong Kong. Then, with a month left in our voyage, we were forced into San Diego for storm repairs. The Treaty of Versailles had restricted naval construction to such a degree that we could not build a decent ship. A hull crack two inches wide. Embarrassing to think the American Naval Yard had to take us in.

It would not happen again. The Führer had seen to it. He signed an agreement with the English that defied the wretched treaty and its limits on our navy. More men, more surface ships. More submarines.

Suddenly it was submarines that fired my imagination. Within months we had a flotilla of U-boats, the first since the last war. And Karl Dönitz for commander of the *U-Bootwaffe*—a brilliant choice.

During the nine months of formal classes at our *Marineschule Mürwik*, my mind fixed on one day commanding a U-boat. Through every class from navigation to weaponry to maritime law—yes even the gentlemanly instruction in fencing, horseback riding, and dancing—I pictured myself behind the arms of a periscope.

A romantic lure for a midshipman who still had much to learn. Like the men of any crew, I was sent to sea in other ships to learn the seaman's trade. First the steamer *Hecht* to learn navigation. Then the cruiser *Nürnberg* to take on the duties of radio operator. When our soldiers were marching through Poland we were patrolling the Baltic, and, within weeks, covering our destroyers in the North Sea while they laid mines off the coast of England.

It was my first proof of the potency of the submarine. Even if this one belonged to the Royal Navy. The enemy unleashed a torpedo that struck the bow of the *Nürnberg,* and sent the ship limping back to Kiel. No one had laid eyes on the submarine. It slithered into firing distance and slithered away again. A formless huntsman, a clever, artful magician. My imagination solidified. One day I would command an iron rogue.

HAROLD WALKS OFF INTO THE DARKNESS. FOR A MOMENT Taverner stares vacantly after him, before refilling his mind with other, more urgent matters. The passengers delivered their lives into his hands the minute they set foot on the gangplank in North Sydney. The least they expect is to be delivered safely to the other side.

There are captains who will assert it's all in God's hands. Taverner is not one of them. He'll take the weight of it, frustrated by what he sees as the Canadian Navy hanging back, juggling the load. He'll brood on it, only for a time, then take charge and do what must be done. The *Caribou* is his ship after all.

The vessel took its name from the symbol of the Royal Newfoundland Regiment. It memorializes the regiment's enormous loss in the Great War.

Newfoundlanders dealt with the Germans before and now they are having to deal with them again. Can it be any more than a matter of time? To Taverner, believing otherwise defies common sense.

On September 3rd the *Donald Stewart*, loaded with fuel and cement for the construction of the American air base in Labrador, was sunk. That, Taverner told his son, was common sense, on the part of the Germans.

Harold slips back next to his father, as silently as when he left. He confirms that the lifeboats are in order. Two of the three, port and starboard, are swung out on their davits, as the Captain instructed. The Carley rafts have been inspected and are ready to be deployed.

Harold is sounding well versed. He reports that the escort ship, the *Grandmère*, is keeping a steady pace.

That Taverner knows full well. He knows, too, that neither ship is equipped with wireless, that they are silent, mismatched partners.

Harold is not concerned. His optimism, his father long ago concluded, was learned during his time on the Great Lakes.

Taverner himself is known to be optimistic, when he has reason for it. But neither is he used to relying on hope. It's not his habit.

Into the lounge of the *Caribou* waltzes John, suitcases in hand, two Nursing Sisters tight behind him. One is rather too severe to set a fire under the steward, but the other is a sweet good-looker, the catch of the trip. Not that John is about to have his instincts unleashed, not as long as he's on duty and Bride is in charge.

John suggests they take a seat while he gets the matter of their accommodation straightened out. He chooses a table and pulls out a chair for each of them.

Bride has other ideas. Mrs. Shiers and her baby need to be shown to their cabin.

John hardly bats an eye. He assures the two nurses that he'll be back directly. Which he will, at all costs.

John gathers up the woman's bag and heads off with her and young Leonard, following her thank-you and thank-you again to Lundrigan. The man has already turned his thoughts to settling into the lounge for the night.

Bride's concern for him hasn't dissipated, but Lundrigan assures her he'll be comfortable enough. She looks over at Hank and Buzz, ensconced at the piano, and reminds them that the lounge closes at midnight. Earlier, if it gets rowdy. Bride has been known to shut it down prematurely on more than one occasion.

Hank's hand is in Lundrigan's like a shot. 'Hank Scheller, sir, U.S. Army Air Corps, heading back to base in Stephenville.'

'William Lundrigan, building contractor.' His company has been doing a lot of work in Stephenville. 'It's a pleasure to meet you.'

Hank's attention is divided. The younger, prettier nurse has removed her raglan and settled in at the table. Hank, as Bride notes, is feeling something of a stir.

He's about to turn back to Lundrigan but glances over at the table again. He wonders aloud where she's headed. To his neck of the woods, if he's lucky.

He's not so lucky. 'Wrong uniform,' Bride informs him, not without a smile. The two nurses are Canadian and on their way to the naval hospital in St. John's.

'Nevertheless,' Hank says, 'I do love a woman in uniform.' Any uniform.

I'm sure you do, Bride thinks. And out of one, too.

The nurses introduce themselves to Bride. One is Charlotte, the other Martha. Martha has been in Manitoba and Charlotte in Saskatchewan, on leave and back home for a few weeks.

Hank is charmed and pulls another chair to the table, seating himself backwards in one slick motion. Sa-skat-che-wan. It stutters off his tongue, though his accent maintains a certain allure. And she misses it terribly?

For the moment Charlotte holds her distance. She is not so

easily won over. 'Yes, it's the prairies, and it's home.' But she and Martha have chosen to make sacrifices and are happy doing so.

'We make do,' Martha insists. She inquires if Hank is American, her derision not well disguised.

It fails to register. Hank smiles broadly.

There is a measure of sweet nostalgia in Charlotte's voice that she has not been able to completely exclude. What she misses most are the skies, the huge prairie skies, skies that stretch on forever.

Lundrigan steps closer. 'The ocean then. You must enjoy the ocean. When it's flat calm and the sun's going down. There's nothing more big and beautiful.'

Hank is out in the cold for the moment.

Martha breathes it in. Certainly, both nurses love Newfoundland, it being such an interesting place with the war on and all. Even though it is overrun with soldiers at the moment.

Hank has found the lead he's been groping for. He's proud to declare that Uncle Sam has been giving the island a much-needed economic boost.

Lundrigan sets him straight. Newfoundland is the first line of defense if Hitler sets his sights on the United States. In which case it'll be Newfoundland paying the price.

'No need to worry,' Hank insists. 'President Roosevelt will be shipping G.I.s off to Europe by the thousands. We'll be taking care of Hitler soon enough.' And in the meantime, what about having ourselves a little fun?

On Hank's intake of breath, Buzz sets the ivories dancing.

Hank offers up a Coke for each of the nurses. Martha declines. Charlotte, on the other hand, shows no such reluctance.

Charlotte is missing the prairie, but, apparently, so is the Texan.

He sidles up to the piano, cutting into Buzz's line at exactly the right spot.

The stars at night are big and bright
Deep in the heart of Texas
The prairie sky is wide and high…

If at first she was at odds to show it, Charlotte is now suitably enamored. She gradually eases herself into the four-beat refrain, clapping along smartly and in faultless rhythm.

That first patrol came in May of 1941, aboard U-74, Eitel-Friedrich Kentrat in command. I was first watch officer, his right-hand man.

We were there when the *Bismarck* fell beneath the waves.

We heard it underwater, as we stood motionless in the control room, the rumble and hideous crack of hull iron bending to the pressure. For the moment we lived in hope it was an enemy ship, but that hope quickly vanished. We had been ordered to attack what British ships we could, but when finally we broke the surface, the ships had gone. All that remained was a sea strewn with debris, its waves lapping over dead bodies wrapped in yellow life-vests. The enemy had lowered ropes over the sides of their vessels and taken aboard a hundred men before abandoning the rest. Two thousand German sailors drowned with the sinking of the *Bismarck*. We searched for a day and found three clinging to a raft, barely alive. That was all, until our orders came. We abandoned the dead and made for home.

On the way, the three men revived enough to tell their story. There had been a fourth, a war correspondent, who was lost when the raft capsized. He and his bundle of film. I have often wondered if he had his camera running when the ship was under attack, if there might have been a record of the savagery. More savage than the attack on the *Hood*, more savage by 700 German lives.

This war is a war of numbers. For us to sink ships in numbers faster than the enemy can build them. For them to sink ours faster than we can build our own. Numbers quickened by cunning, by the clever stroke of luck.

I learnt this on that very first patrol as we made our way into the Bay of Biscay, within reach of Lorient. Damaged batteries kept us on the surface except for the briefest of dives and, to no one's surprise, an English submarine spotted us. As first watch officer, I and my vigilant trio of men had the most crucial of the watches—in daylight, when we are most visible. The four of us positioned against the railing of the bridge, each responsible for a quadrant, each pair of eyes sealed to the deadweight of his Zeiss, slowly scanning the surface, back and forth, as precise as humanly possible. Arms ached after a time, eyes lost their focus, so there was a quick moment when I let the binoculars hang by the straps and stretched my arms about, arched my back before raising them to my eyes once again. There was not much said between us. We made a good watch, serious when we needed to be. It was very far from the future, playful, sun-drenched watches in the West Indies, jazz music filtering up through the hatch.

This watch was coldly somber. I felt the burden, and when, for a moment, I lost concentration, I silently cursed my inadequacy. From time to time the captain appeared on the bridge, saying nothing to distract us, not even resting a hand on my shoulder as he might do in a less crucial situation, prelude to recounting an incident from another patrol. He, like myself, could taste the meager distance to the safety of Lorient, yet knew the stories of U-boats fooled into thinking themselves past the threat of the Tommies.

He left the last stretch to us, but he was gone only a few seconds when something caught my eye.

'Alarm!'

Immediately the three others dropped straight down the hatch, one after the other, without setting foot on the ladder. The first to land had to immediately fling himself out of the way of the man dropping behind him, and that man out of the way of the next. I was last, jerking to a stop on the ladder just long enough to pull the hatch cover closed behind me. Not before a torrent of seawater cascaded over my head.

I turned the wheel on the hatch, dropped the last few feet, sopping wet. The ship was at an impossibly sharp angle, diving as quickly as the engines could thrust us below.

There was a moment when I gripped the captain's arm, to keep myself upright, and to punish through the few seconds until we both could breathe again.

'The first two missed us.' There was several moments' hesitation. 'And now the other four.'

None of us could believe there had been a sweep of six torpedoes.

'The bastard is desperate.'

We levelled out and veered in another direction.

In good time the captain gave orders to bring us to the surface once again. I raced up the ladders to the bridge, the other three behind me. There was no sign of the Tommy. Either he gave up in frustration or had run out of torpedoes. In either case we made a desperate run for Lorient, with all the speed the engine room could deliver. A minesweeper met us, then led us past the fortifications of Port-Louis, into the inner harbour.

The tension fell away only when we made it to safety, the quay and the bunkers in clear sight. Word of our arrival preceded us and a smart collection of gay young nurses, holding flowers, cheered and waved as a military band festooned the air with a robust, triumphant march. It was a homecoming out of proportion to our achievement, but we carried men from the *Bismarck,* and it was those three who overwhelmed the moment. They were the ones the reporters had come to interview, before they were whisked away to Paris. U-74's crew was duly welcomed by one of the navy subordinates. After all, we had not sunk a single ship.

John emerges from below deck. In the lounge he stops abruptly, left on the outside looking in. He's determined not to remain there for long. His sights have been preset on Charlotte, who is more than pleased to tell him that Hank is from Texas, and that Texans have a wonderful accent.

The steward shrugs. There is a pause while his smile contracts.

The G.I. eagerly steps into the picture. His accent thicker than ever, he invites John to sit and have a drink with them. John, stiff with self-doubt, hesitates. In any case Bride intercedes, reminding the steward that he's on duty, that consumption of alcohol is absolutely against regulations. She has overstated her case.

He doesn't drink Coke, John tells Hank, with a decisiveness out of proportion to the situation. He turns back to Charlotte, and now Martha. He's the attentive, efficient steward, extending an invitation to lead them to their cabin. Martha stands up immediately. Charlotte doesn't and Hank's got a song for her, a new Cole Porter tune. 'Not many people know it yet,' according to Hank, 'but it's a great tune for a prairie girl like yourself.'

Oh, give me land, lots of land, under starry skies above...

Bride is not about to stand by and watch the young steward plummet pitifully from grace. John's way with a song is not to be dismissed. He has been known to do a wonderful rendition of "The Petty Harbour Bait Skiff."

Hank wonders aloud if Bing might be interested in recording it? Or the Andrews Sisters? Charlotte loves the Andrews Sisters. And so does Bride.

John groans in his struggle to keep his head above water. And now it's Lundrigan's turn to come to his aid. He declares that music is in the blood of every Newfoundlander. He turns to John, having laid open the opportunity for the steward to redeem himself. The young man launches forth.

Good people all, both great and small, I hope you will attend
And listen to these verses few that I have lately penned
And I'll relate the hardships great that fishermen must stand...

He sings well enough, and with an admirable intensity, but it doesn't get him far in the competition for the innocent Charlotte.

'Rather grim,' Hank suggests. Perhaps John could come up with something a bit more lively. More party-like. Charlotte does love a piano. Buzz jumps in on cue.

Bride turns to John, figuring to save what's left of his self-esteem. 'There's no time to sit and listen. The Nursing Sister is anxious to get to her cabin.' With a suitcase in each hand and Martha to lead him out the door, John slowly exits the lounge, deflated. Not a second too quickly.

Buzz is in high gear and Hank redoubles his enthusiasm for Cole Porter.

Oh, give me land, lots of land under starry skies above
Don't fence me in.
Let me ride through the wide open country that I love...

As John heads to the stairs it's Charlotte he hears, suddenly eager to sing along. And, as Bride sees it, there's not a fence in sight.

I FIRST SAW THE YOUNG WOMAN ON THE QUAY, AND SHE seemed to pay the crew little attention beyond the staged gaiety of the welcome given every U-boat upon its return. Then I caught her looking my way, though I knew better than to let my eyes linger, given the untidy growth of beard and the concoction of smells produced by fifty men clumped together for four weeks. Fresh air alone was not about to erase it. The nurses trooped along the quay in single file to present their flowers, each lovely in her own way, in stylish, slim-fitting suits, hair carefully set in roll waves and curls. I smiled and bowed. '*Fräulein*.' She returned the smile and moved on.

I knew to keep a distance, until, freshly laundered, I could regenerate myself for the outside world. A submariner has his life aboard his U-boat and his life ashore, and when the two intersect, he is never anything but a misfit.

The return to land had its order. First the gathering in what had once been an assembly hall of the French *préfecture*. Mail was laid on a long stretch of tables joined together and covered with white linen tablecloths. I would come to know this ceremony several times, and still I would never be prepared for the emotional morass that would unfold. Bundles, neatly tied, large and small, had been lined along the length of the tables, one for each man. Some amounted to a dozen letters and more, several lay atop packages. A few were but a single envelope. For two men there were none at all. During the next while, we were left alone while we devoted ourselves to the mail. I preferred to take my bundle and escape to a corner.

My letters were mostly from my parents in Dresden, writing separately, as was their habit. The doctor's was full of praise for the path I had chosen. He was anxious to hear of my first patrol, unlike my mother, who wanted only word that I was safe and well. The doctor was quick to direct my attention to hardships the city was enduring, though in the same breath he began a detailed account of a Pfitzner concert at the Semperoper. He loves music above all else. Pfitzner is his favourite, more so than Strauss, far beyond Wagner. A relative of Karl Böhm, conductor at the Semperoper, is a patient of his and it has made his devotion to the concert season all the more intense.

I turned to other letters, my mother's handwriting in contrast to the doctor's weighted scratch. Hers was smallish, and florid, if incompletely so, diminished from what I knew of it as a cadet away from home. It seemed to hold the burden of her worry. Her words only heightened it.

My mother's life had fallen into itself. She has a gossipy sister, whom I knew would be of no help, and a brother she adores but who lives in Munich, too far away to share the strain. The good doctor had a limit to his sympathy. I loved my mother and would be quick to write and reassure her that I couldn't have been happier than I was at this moment, my first patrol behind me, the next a few weeks away.

Five weeks to be exact. But in the meantime there was life to be lived and Elise came to be at the centre of it.

Before the tryst that began the relationship, there were other matters demanding attention. Matters beyond the opening of mail—to begin, a banquet with the Flotilla staff to celebrate our safe return. The *Kriegsmarine* spares no expense in showing its gratitude to the men it casts out into the Atlantic. We might survive the patrol on stale eggs cooked a hundred different ways, each paired with stagnant sauerkraut, but once we strike dry land, food choices are seemingly endless—sausages, hams, goose, duck, fresh fruit and vegetables, caviar and champagne. A prelude to a night among the ladies of Lorient.

The regular man had his fill along the street they laughingly called *Der Staße der Bewegung*. I had the guidance of a gentleman of the Flotilla staff whose role it was to discretely steer U-boat officers away from the common dens to a place more in keeping with their rank. It was June and, in the twilight, the tall, dense border of blue hydrangea overflowing the walkway gave the excursion a rightly civil air. The colour fixed in my mind and it was that colour, more so than what followed, that remained there.

'*Oberleutnant* Gräf, you will not be disappointed. Madame has them well in hand. They know the art of fucking.'

The gentleman suddenly thought of us as long-standing companions where rank had fallen away, replaced by a mutual, outright thirst for sex. I suggested he leave me to my own devices, now that the entrance door was in sight. He thought it part of his role to join me for the evening. I insisted I was perfectly fine and hung my hand momentarily on his shoulder. He retreated, his disappointment turning to irritation before he was properly out of sight.

I would eventually report back to him that Madame lived up to his expectations. Her girls likely exceeded them.

'*Oberleutnant*,' she said, holding my hand, once my uniform had been interpreted, 'I have been expecting you.' She was plump and shimmering in her purple satin dress and matching scarf of a Chinese brocade. Her hair was coiffured in a rigid balance worthy of the most expensive brothel in Paris. She smoothed my hand with her own, its multitude of rings looking as if they couldn't possibly be dislodged from the ridges of flesh. I took to her immediately.

'Madame, you should be so kind.' I bowed slightly. 'U-boatmen are forever appreciative of a steady hand, to offset the uncertainty still in our legs.' With a quiet, liquored smile.

'Young man, you have chosen a place where upright steadiness is the least concern. Come, have a little champagne, join us on the parlour couches. The girls adore a fresh face, and yours is as untarnished as any they have seen in weeks.' She withdrew her hand from mine and touched it to my cheeks.

The parlour was separated from its ante-chamber by a heavy curtain of an embossed, wine-coloured velvet. Madame parted it to allow me inside, then, as I walked through, let it fall back in place behind me. I stood alone and for the moment unnoticed. It was an abrupt beginning. Filling the couches were couples in various states of entanglement, viewing a film that indeed portrayed the art of fucking. It was a poorly focused training film shot through gossamer, awkwardly attempting to retain some dignity. It did leave something to the imagination, although not a great deal.

'Let the sweet fucker have his way!' yelled a drunken officer I might have recognized had not the girl encircling him so quickly held her hand over his mouth. The establishment had its rules. A ban on vulgar commentary was one of them.

The evening proceeded as expected. Before long I, too, occupied the couch, a girl—Josette and all of eighteen—doing her business so to speak, leading me to a half hour in a separate, if ungainly narrow, room. It fulfilled the promise of the hydrangea. I left with Madame's hand once again against my face.

'Young man,' she said, 'may you forever have such a face.'

Not the thing to have said to a U-boatman.

As Hank sees it, a fellow lives in hope that his last night on leave will put a glow where it matters most. Hank doesn't yet think of himself as a ladies' man, but he's all for trying, and, since taking up his posting in Newfoundland, it's landed the Texan in some promising places.

He knows the Southern Baptist folks back in Abilene might take exception, but there it is. The army has a way of firing a fellow up on all cylinders. He looks at Charlotte and sees a definite possibility. He would argue that Canada hasn't put anything prettier in uniform.

An airman like himself can't be counting one month to the next. This month it's Newfoundland, but come November he could be dropping bombs on Hitler's doorstep. An airman takes the orders handed to him and whistles while he walks away to suit up, the music of a good time ringing in his ears.

Hank is all smiles at how easily Buzz works the piano. He can see that Charlotte has a thirst for music and his mind is wild with speculation at how that same thirst might just make its way on over to him.

Let me ride through the wide open country that I love…

Charlotte is quick to play her part. *Don't fence me in…*

In John's mind there are Yanks, and then there are Yanks.

He got to know both kinds in St. Anthony where he grew up and where he worked for the Grenfell Mission, and in New York, where the Mission sent him for training in machine repair. The fellow he buddied around with in New York he liked as well as anyone he's ever met.

Hank is the first Texan he's come across. He figures if he's the last, that would suit him fine.

John runs into Alex, another steward, who calls him a sore loser. It rubs John the wrong way. A sensible girl like Charlotte—he figured she'd spot a blowhard when she saw one.

Alex appreciates the spirit in the fellow. It reminds him of himself when he was John's age. Alex is older by two decades, but they've become decent friends since John started work aboard the *Caribou*.

They show up in the lounge, where Buzz is still pumping out the tunes. Alex is impressed. He hasn't heard anyone work that piano so well in a very long time.

John nods reluctantly. His eyes are on Hank, with Charlotte next to him as he leans into the piano.

You leave the Pennsylvania Station 'bout a quarter to four
Read a magazine and then you're in Baltimore

There are couples carving up the floor, swing dancing. Hank suddenly halts his singing to lead Charlotte by the hand and into the midst of them, polishing off a few fancy maneuvers.

The second they return to the piano Charlotte pitches in with the chorus.

Chattanooga choo choo!
Won't you choo-choo, choo-choo, choo-choo me home!

John huffs his disapproval. He looks Hank straight in the eye and imagines a fist sending his Yankee ass sailing back across the dance floor.

John might think it, but that's as far as it goes. He has no intention of ending up in Bride's bad books.

At that moment, the woman herself enters the lounge.

Charlotte presses her hand hesitantly over Hank's.

A final groan emanates from John, barely audible. He turns in Bride's direction and smiles.

A FEW MOMENTS OF PRIVATE CONVERSATION WITH ELISE and all thoughts of ever revisiting Madame and her girls vanished. We met the next day, during the course of a stop at the hospital with young Otto from the engine room who had twisted his knee while on patrol. He was examined, assured that the damage was not permanent, and given crutches.

While he spent time with the doctor I sought out the nurse, whom I had caught a glimpse of when I first entered the hospital. I interrupted her walk through the corridor. 'Excuse me.'

She didn't look to be in a particular hurry, yet she hesitated to stop. 'Yes?'

'May I ask your name?'

It seemed to strike her as odd, perhaps insolent. Of course it had nothing to do with her being a nurse, yet my rank was not to be ignored.

'Perhaps you do not recognize me without the beard?' I said, to give her more time. 'The haircut?'

'Yes, *Oberleutnant* Gräf.'

'And *your* name?'

'Elise.'

'And shall we meet, then, over dinner perhaps?'

U-boatmen learn from the start that time, above all else, is harboured. It is not to be squandered on preamble.

She was not surprised. And if hesitant, not for long. As long as it took to offer her full name. I had no restaurant in mind. She knew better than I what Lorient had to offer.

She chose a restaurant along *Passage de la Comédie*. Filled mostly with local patrons who by now were used to the presence of Germans in their town, and to their money. The verbose welcome and the platter of seafood, as good as it was—and with the French it is never anything but very good—is not what I most recall about the evening. It is the candlelight on the contours of her face, the warm intelligence it revealed, the way the light caught her blue-green eyes, the way they came to hold for seconds with mine, unwillingly at first, but, before the dinner ended, with more promise than I could have anticipated.

I was of a mind to fall in love. At twenty-five I'd had no more than an incidental fling that fell away to nothing when I returned to *Marineschule*. Months aboard training ships led nowhere that befitted the uniform. Various ports offered various escapes and little more than a good story to share when the nights at sea grew tedious. Elise held in me the hope that I had found something infinitely more pleasing, that, given the chance, there could unfold a relationship that would lead to places of the heart I had never known. I was desperate for that to happen, though I knew enough to keep my thoughts to myself.

Elise was three years younger, not that it mattered. She came from Munich. I remembered as a child visiting the city and my uncle taking me to the *Christkindlesmarkt*. She assured me the holiday market had continued despite the war. Odd, such talk, but perhaps it is talk of childhood, where memories are strongest and most at peace, that deepens a bond.

We spoke of other things, of course, though nothing of my time aboard the U-boat. It was as if it were forbidden territory, as if to speak of it would bring the danger closer and spoil the evening. She did not want to be thinking of such things when the cocoon we had made for ourselves, at the corner table in *Le Grand Café de l'Univers,* was ours alone, shielded from all the world outside.

What else mattered then but the falling in love? Nothing at that moment, and little else for the few weeks ashore until it was time to re-board U-74. We spent them together as much as we could. It seemed never predictable what time there would be for each other, for Elise was at the beck and call of the head nurse, and when a U-boat arrived in Lorient it was never known beforehand what emergencies might await the hospital staff. We had our favourite meeting spots in the city centre, and we had our share of moments, and sometimes when least anticipated, which made them all the better.

Once she arrived unexpectedly at our *Hôtel Beauséjour,* where some of the U-boat officers were quartered, on the pretense of relaying a message to me from one of the doctors. There were few men about since most were on leave with their families. Only those who like myself had duties still in Lorient.

Obersteuermann Metz called me to the foyer, unable to contain his smirk as he passed me on his way to the hotel's brasserie. Elise was embarrassed by her own boldness. I was delighted by it, and quickly proposed a walk. We left together, not knowing exactly where we were headed. She still could not believe what she had done, and suddenly, having glanced back, opened a gap between us. I looked back myself to find Metz standing on the front step with his cigarette, now with his hand raised to me.

Her reticence only eased when we had turned the corner into the next street. She finally slowed her pace, enough that our conversation lost its urgency. I offered my arm and we walked on, and to the casual passer-by we might have looked a seasoned couple, out for an evening promenade.

She was in truth unsettled, but I held my other hand against hers in the crook of my arm, talking all the while, about nothing of importance, but with enthusiasm exaggerated enough that she forgot herself for the moment. We could have been in some provincial German town, two companions on the cusp of love, about to embark on an intriguing adventure to further seal their affair.

It was not far off the truth. That evening we strolled *Cours de la Bôve*, past the statue of Lorient's own Victor Massé, then seated ourselves on one of the park benches that lined the centre concourse. I proposed we escape for a day to Larmor-Plage, just a few kilometers from Lorient, and with claims of being one of the best expanses of sandy beach in all Brittany.

She protested that we hardly knew each other, that she had plans for her weekly day off duty, that what if she were seen and the head nurse got wind of the escapade? All excuses that I cheerfully dismissed one by one, for which she had no counter argument, none at least she cared to raise. By which time her head had fallen against my shoulder and I would be willing to bet she was already planning her wardrobe for the day.

What I most remember of that wardrobe was the green polka-dot swimsuit and the woman that filled it so favourably. I could hardly comprehend my good fortune—a woman I met but a few days before stretched with me across the sand, so delicious in that swimsuit. Elise and I were a promising pair.

I ran into the ocean, calling over my shoulder for her to join me. Waist-deep in the water, I devoured the sight of her walking toward me, self-reliant, smiling modestly. I drew her toward me in a playful embrace, her bare skin against mine. I could hardly contain my eagerness, but she wasn't about to give in so freely.

It was peculiar filling myself up in the ocean, when I lived to hold that same ocean at bay, the last thing a U-boatman should ever want of saltwater. The fearsome enemy beyond the hatch, its horizon line wavering with the crosshairs of the periscope. A deadly playing field, the same one now immersing me in the other great passion, as if they could blend, somehow, one with the other.

We returned to Lorient at the end of the day. I kissed her good night, before leaving her to walk the remainder of the way alone to her hospital residence. I couldn't get enough of that kiss, the nearest I could come to burying myself in the whole of her, all the while my imagination running wildly past the moment. She drew back, both our spirits magnified, but left at the brink, kept for another day.

'Good night,' she said, and held her fingers against my lips, holding in the pleasure, my smile all that was left before she turned and walked on.

'Good night.'

The boat is settling down. The children have been stowed away for the night, with only the occasional tired cry behind a cabin door. There are eleven of them aboard and fortunately the ship is due a smooth sail.

A trio of sailors from the Royal Navy jostle along the hallway in the direction of the lounge. Bride nods their way. She bids them a good evening and reminds them there are babies being put to sleep still, that the lounge closes at midnight. They are welcome to enjoy themselves, within her limits.

There are no troublemakers among them, as far as Bride can tell. Some nights Bride is more bouncer than stewardess. A fist might fly once, but it won't a second time.

Every half hour she makes her rounds, sees to it that everyone is satisfied as far as they can be satisfied. The dining room has closed its doors. That will send another batch of passengers off for the night. All exterior lights have been dead since the ship left North Sydney. Windows are sealed tight with blackout curtains.

Even so, the war can seem very far away until she hears the stories. Bride knows the three she just passed all have stories, have seen things they wouldn't want to see again, have all lost friends, maybe even stared death in the face themselves. She won't be the one to ask. They're about to sit around the lounge with a few drinks, and are not there to be reminded.

She calls into the bridge to see how the captain is doing, to see if she can get him a hot cup of tea if nothing else. She feels her way there more than use her eyesight. The bridge is lit only by the moon.

Bride first heard of Captain Ben Taverner in 1927, in New York. The year Lindbergh was all the rage, flying non-stop from New York to Paris. The world had gone wild for aviation and the *New York Daily Mirror* wasn't missing out on a chance to boost its circulation. Owner William Randolph Hearst offered $25,000 to anyone who could fly non-stop from New York to Rome. In September a Fokker monoplane with two crewmen and the newspaper's editor came crashing down in the Atlantic, 350 miles east of Newfoundland. No trace could be found. Not until Hearst hired the *Kyle* and Captain Ben to search for the missing plane. Against all odds, the Captain found the wreckage, 100 miles northeast of where everyone was telling him the plane went down. The man has an incredible mind for wind and ocean currents.

The following year he took command of the *Caribou*. He has been a fixture aboard her ever since. He knows his vessel like the back of either one of his hefty hands. As Bride has often quipped, he knows her better than he knows his own family.

That would be his wife, Millie, and seven children, five boys and two girls. There was another boy, the first, who died in infancy. It's only what Bride has heard. The captain would never be the one to tell her.

Even though Bride has never been a mother herself, she often thinks about the captain's wife. Three of her men on the same ship. She must be worried sick, Bride believes, yet the captain would have all five of their sons aboard if he could have managed it.

And she considers Mrs. Lundrigan. Twelve children, and not even Catholic. They must have a saint for a mother. And Lundrigan a saint for a wife, putting up with him.

Bride's parents only ever had the one child. And long ago Bride herself decided she'd want the same, no matter who she might marry. A child to keep her company in her old age. Not that she has anything against children. Not that anyone has ever proposed to her. Gerald likely had it in his mind, but never did get around to it.

The captain is six foot tall, and there's no mistaking him, even in the dark. He recognizes her voice. He assures her he's not in need of anything. One of the kitchen staff came by earlier.

It's a calm night, they both agree. She can tell right away when Taverner is not himself, even when he's no more than a vague outline across the way.

Calm and clear. Too clear.

Bride is one of the few Taverner allows into his confidence. It wasn't always that way, but gradually, over the many years they've been together on the ferry, he and Bride, as the *Caribou* begins to settle down for the night, have taken to having a private few words.

Tonight there is silence. They are both feeling the weight of the trip, and neither wants to be the one to confirm it.

Taverner gives into it first. He questions whether it is worth the risk. For the moment Bride is unsure what to say.

The captain she thought she knew would not be the one to question crossing the Strait. He crosses it over and back three times a week, every week.

Bride wonders aloud just how many military men the *Caribou* has carried since the war began. Thousands. Many of them have gone overseas. And many of them won't be coming back. Just like they never came back from the last war. Carrying them across the Strait is the least they can do.

The silence resumes, taking on a clearer pitch.

Millie finds it hard to sleep when he's at sea, Taverner tells her, especially the past few weeks.

Bride keeps the attention where she believes it belongs. She recites several names her mother has mentioned in her letters. Men from Bay Roberts where Bride grew up, gone off to war, some lying about their age. Some who'll never see home again.

The crew aboard the ferry all have their parts to play.

That's what it's all about. That's why they're here.

Even the passengers have their parts.

From the bridge nothing much can be seen, unless there's someone with sharper eyes than Bride's. A pale cast of sea is all, in moonlight an undulating, fractured grey. If there is anything reassuring it is the unflinching propulsion through the water, the vessel cutting consistently into the hollow of night. They are on a path to Newfoundland, and they expect they'll be there before dawn.

Bride wishes the captain had found more to say, but Taverner ends their nightly meeting in the way he has always done. He wishes her good night, with the invocation that God keep her safe.

Bride has her faith, but not enough to satisfy her.

She wishes him good night and tells him to be sure to get some rest, in the way she, too, has always done.

Bride is gone then, thoughts of the captain clinging to her. She is needed in the lounge.

There's another three sailors ahead of her. Newfoundlanders, by the accents. There's only one place they could be headed. She leads the way.

Rum, they tell her, they're devils for the rum.

Rightly so, she thinks.

A man sets his mind to it and he takes his chances.

Sam had said it as John was leaving home, said it when he took him aside, looked him square in the eyes and shook his hand goodbye. He said it as if a man's life depended on it.

His father, Johnny Gilbert, the man whose name he bore, was a sniper, famous in the Newfoundland Regiment for killing dozens of Turks in Gallipoli. John was a few months old when his father died. Sam never would tell him how it happened, how his father, Sam's best friend, was killed.

Sam Kennedy had come home from the war, eventually searched out his best friend's girl and, in the end, married her. Another instance, John concluded, of a steady mind and luck.

Years before John left St. Anthony the urge to get away had started to gnaw at him. He had finished training in New York, had his job with the Grenfell Mission and more than enough reason to stay. He had his mother, Sam, his friends. More often than not, a girl, though never one he liked well enough that he wanted to spend the rest of his life with her. He needed to see more of the world.

That's how he came to be aboard the *Caribou*. He got restless.

Buzz has called it a night. It was a fine time while it lasted, but Buzz is a man who knows his limits. He needs sleep while his buddy, Hank, needs time on his own to take care of business.

Hank has taken over the piano bench, is fiddling with the keys and humming the last tune Buzz played before he left. Charlotte sits next to him, equally relaxed after their dancing, in her navy blue tunic with its double line of brass buttons, white collar and cuffs. She is mildly chagrined by whatever Hank is whispering in her ear.

John shows up and stands to one side of the piano, hands in his trouser pockets until he has Charlotte's attention. He has a message from Martha. Charlotte is about to say something, but John states his case. Her friend Martha is settled away in their cabin. She's hoping Charlotte wouldn't be long.

Hank's eyes intensify. Charlotte puts her hand on one of his and leads it back to the piano keys. John doesn't move, although he is barely able to bring his resentment under control.

Lundrigan, who has been observing it all, calls him over to the table he is sharing with Alex. It manages to disarm the situation.

Alex puts it to him. 'Why haven't you joined up?' Alex missed out on the last war because he was too young and is bound to miss out on this one because he's too old.

As Lundrigan sees it, they're both doing their part, each man in his own way.

Alex grew up a fisherman. When he was John's age, the farthest he strayed from home was the Grand Banks, fishing in an open boat, year after year. And now here he is, three times a week, going all the way to Nova Scotia. He strikes the table with his open palm and chuckles, and reminds John that there are sailors aboard the ship who've been to Gibraltar, to India, to the Suez Canal, that no one gets a real taste of the war staying in Newfoundland.

There's no need. It's already been implanted in John's mind. A fellow needs to get away, even if it is only to size up where he came from.

'The Royal Navy. Join up, or you might live to regret it.'

Lundrigan is not convinced.

'Sir, if you were John's age, you'd be standing in the recruiting line and ready to sign the papers, just as quick as the next fellow.'

'Not if I had a job helping the war effort.'

Alex is not about to force the issue, except for a parting shot—'The women go nuts for fellows in uniform.'

John is certain now. He welcomed the prod that forced him to make up his mind. He'd been hanging on the fence for too long. It's time he stopped being a weak-willed pushover on the outside looking in. It's time he got on with it.

Bride enters the lounge, looks around, assessing the situation. It's nearing midnight. She takes a chair between Lundrigan and Alex, her bulk alighting on the seat as gracefully as she can manage, relieved to be off her feet. The boat is quiet enough. Bride is finally willing to show some sign of relaxing.

Just as she sits down, Hank closes the cover over the piano keys. He stands, a pensive Charlotte tight to his arm.

Her cabin or his—it's the question on the minds of all four seated at the table. The answer will depend on whether Hank can convince Buzz to vacate their room in favour of the lounge.

It's a scene of lame pretense. Hank bids everyone a cheery good night, as does Charlotte, who sets a modest distance between herself and the G.I.

Bride sends an equally cheery response in their direction. She can't resist. 'Sleep tight.'

John huffs, without bothering to look their way as they stroll out the door.

Bride turns to him, 'She's not your type.'

John figures he doesn't have a type.

The conversation is in need of redirection. 'The Royal Navy then?' says Lundrigan. 'Or is it the Canadian Navy?'

'Neither one.' John has kept it to himself until now. No, once the ferry docks in Port aux Basques he'll be boarding the train for St. John's. 'I'm heading straight for the Royal Air Force.' He glances around the table to catch their reactions.

They think him unrealistic, that he'd never get a look-in. But it's the picture that's been in his head and stayed there. Flight Lieutenant John Gilbert. It's been there since he got talking to men from the Newfoundland Squadron of the RAF who'd been aboard the ship a few weeks earlier.

On the crest of the Newfoundland Squadron 125 is a caribou. Every time John walks past the ship's caribou statue, with someone's suitcase in his hand, or a tray of drinks, he has the notion he could be part of that squadron. Perhaps not a pilot. Maybe navigator or gunner. The scenario has been playing constantly in his head.

Bride had no idea.

Lundrigan has his doubts, but he won't be the one to dampen the young fellow's enthusiasm. 'A man can do anything he sets his mind to,' which Lundrigan believes, if not whole-heartedly in this case.

As for Bride, she feigns upset at the fact that it will leave her with no one to take his place on the next trip. That she had it in her mind John would work his way up to head steward one day, after Alex has his run at it.

It's all a game, Alex has decided. 'John has the itch to go, so let him go.' And everyone knows Bride has no intention of retiring. He's been learning to live with that for years.

Meanwhile, it's past midnight. The lounge is closed. It wouldn't be unusual for them all to have a small rum and Coca-Cola on the house before heading off to bed.

Lundrigan shakes his head mildly. Alex has forgotten. The man is a Salvationist and a teetotaler.

In all the ferment, it is Elise who satisfies me. Not Dönitz, not recollections of the doctor, not my mother. Elise fills the toughened heart. The operation of the U-boat fills the mind.

To this point, a fateful patrol. America all but welcomed us with open arms.

U-69 held to periscope depth in clear sight of Chesapeake Bay, Cape Charles to starboard and Cape Henry to port. Overwhelming both, the alien lights of their navy's base at Norfolk. The sounds of detonations unnerved us for the moment, but they proved to be bombing exercises. Powerful searchlights glared across the entrance to the bay.

We dived in any case. We had seen all that needed to be seen.

One of Umbeck's duties was to keep me informed of what Sachse, the soundman, had to offer, not an easy task, given there was no end to the snarl of sounds the man detected through his hydrophones.

We escaped the searchlights, and apparently escaped their SONAR. We settled into the southern part of the sector, where the transmissions drained away. For three hours we quietly dropped our eggs in Chesapeake Bay.

'*Wie ein Lamm, das zur Schlachtbank geführt wird*,' said Hagemann when we had finished and all that was left was to steal away.

Lamb led to the slaughter. He's very good at quoting the Bible, even though he surely doesn't live by it. He prefers the lamb; I prefer the sheep. Sheep silent before its shearers.

We have no way of knowing the consequences of the mines, but are firmly optimistic.

South to Cape Hatteras then, where the Americans made a show of their Zeppelin, so much so we were constantly diving to escape detection. Headquarters gave us the choice and I decided we would head north to see what Canadian waters had to offer.

We slipped into the Gulf of St. Lawrence on the last day of September. On the bridge, the wind stirring a heavy spray, I caught my first sight of Newfoundland.

A U-boat commander knows better than to be lured by the sight of land but nothing had prepared me for the way that hulking rock defied the North Atlantic seas. As if its maker had chiselled breastwork of granite and dared the seas to exhaust themselves against it. This island in all its mockery, this jagged barricade against the unrelenting wind, against the thundery of ocean waves. Sunlight turns any land mass to good, but Newfoundland on a rough day is magnificent, its lofty cliffs indomitable, the surf capable of no more than playing at its feet.

If it were not war, if I were not a navy man, I would walk this island merely to gaze on such a wild, magnificent specimen of nature. I would roam for days, sketchbook at hand, and lose myself in its wilderness.

I have never known wilderness, true primordial wilderness. Yet I would at a moment's call. I would take again to the drawing pencils, in the path of Marc, in his days before Verdun.

For now I must be satisfied to linger at its edge and let the war unfold. I have orders to follow, and patrols to bring to their end.

What quickens me now is the roar of life and death, and that requires every particle of my mind.

The Gulf of St. Lawrence was hardly what I hoped it would be. In daylight our Metox picked up their radar transmissions, kept us clear of the Canadians and their drudging aircraft patrols. We spent as much time below the surface as above. Yet, come nightfall and we had the comforts of a training cruise in the Baltic. We meandered about, hawk-eyed in the murk, in constant faith that something would show itself.

A U-boat commander brings to balance the weights of genesis and destruction. The latter unavoidable if the first is to breathe again.

Many nights Taverner has stood on deck alone, pipe smoke curling into the darkness, the ship's funnels the same, the sea a stern, undulating grey. It was odd comfort. Most men are meant for land, but Taverner moves as the sea moves, makes sense of its troubles, knows when to defy its intemperance. He was never one to fear the sea, though never one to trust it. Some have said it does strange things to the equilibrium of a man.

Not strange, for Taverner's will is fused with the will of the sea, his judgment honed in the steady passage from boy to youth to rough, eager-muscled man.

Bruce, Lintrose, Meigle, Glencoe, Sagona, Kyle, Prospero, Caribou.

These vessels has he captained. Each its own. No two the same. Some coastal boats for a summer and fall, the *Caribou* for these many years. Now a vessel caught in the vagaries of war.

He had always thought himself a fortunate man. Seas he can deal with. Rocks and shoals, wind and ice. There was comfort to be found. He had no enemies.

After nine unproductive days I turned u-69 deeper into the St. Lawrence. No u-boat has ever struck so far into these waters. You would have thought the Canadians would be vigilant enough to put a stop to it.

In our sights on the night of October 9, grid ba 3827, was a convoy of six, three of which we took to be ore carriers. In two columns, each escorted in forward position. Our distance was far from ideal, but the only choice, given that the flank protection of the second column was so near.

We maneuvered to our most promising tract, at 2000 meters.

Blood quickened, dogged years of training fired a need to obliterate those vessels from the sea. Debate annulled, instinct filled my brain.

At 0553 we were pitched to attack. 'Flood tubes one and four. Stand by for surface firing.'

Confirmation returned from the bow compartment through the speaking tube.

Hagemann had ordered the *Überwasserzieloptik* set in place on the bridge, its heavy night binoculars connected by cable through the hatch to the calculator in the tower below. The calculator was connected to the gyrocompass and the torpedoes, the steering adjustments made automatically. Hagemann's job was to keep the target in the crosshairs of the UZO, far from simple considering the distance.

'Starboard, thirty degrees.'

I had every confidence in the first watch officer, bent over the UZO, his concentration at its highest pitch. He swept his right hand upward. 'Open torpedo doors!' He moved the hand to the firing lever.

Through the speaking tube, 'Tube one clear. Tube four clear.'

I called to Hagemann, 'Permission to fire.'

There was a collective intake of breath.

'Tube four—fire!' A halt, and then, 'Tube one—fire!'

A fanning pair of torpedo shots.

'Hard a-starboard!' And we were running clear, course fifty degrees.

A wait of four minutes, one detonation. A wait of another minute. The sweet resounding plume of explosion. A freighter—4,000 GRT by my estimation—buried in flames. It broke apart and in two minutes was seeking its grave. The sea swallowed the fire, the enemy ship gone from sight, slumping to the river bottom.

I suspect star shells from the escorts lit the night sky, but U-69 too had slipped beneath the river waters, nothing to be seen. There was no time to glory in the kill.

That came later.

'*Prost*!' Around the meal table, a toast to success, to the first of many, if luck was with us and the Canadians continued their doltish ways.

'*Anfeuerungen*!' The thick glasses jangled again. Beer foam spilled over our hands. They laughed uproariously at Umbeck's choice of word. Umbeck is not known for his sense of humour.

The second watch officer rarely shows much of himself, intimidated by Hagemann, who might be mistaken for a ruffian were it not for his levelheadedness when it counts. This is Umbeck's first commission, assigned to the U-boat by Headquarters without consultation. These days you take who you are given. The training is cut to a fraction of what it was, and there are far fewer men than there were at the start.

Not that I haven't found something to like in the fellow. Umbeck knows his job, if he has trouble convincing himself his is the right way to go about it. Hagemann has no patience with him, bemoaning still the reassignment of Umbeck's predecessor, and his only ally, to another boat. It does neither of the watch officers any good. I've had words with Hagemann, to little effect. Likely even less when I am not in their company.

So Umbeck's half smile and *Anfeuerungen*! gave the rest of us some relief, much needed since our eating quarters are impossibly cramped at the best of times. One or more of the officers are constantly having to stand, step aside and draw in their breath, to allow any coming and going past the table. The oversized cook entered and the space lost half its air. The man farted as he was leaving and the world collapsed.

Hagemann buried himself in his sausage and potato. 'Pig-shit.'

'He's Bavarian. Is there any hope?' said Schieder, our Chief Engineer, known better as Chief.

Hagemann hissed, and they all laughed, Umbeck to the point of raising his glass again, having done well with his first round.

'To Bavarians who shit! *Anfeuerungen*!'

Hagemann shoved his plate aside and left the table, like a petulant schoolboy. All drama of course. He was back five minutes later, as if nothing had happened, as if he was the one deserving an explanation for the sudden pit of silence into which the table had descended.

'Well,' said Hagemann, 'are you all tongue-tied. Go about your foolish business.'

There is never any pleasing the first watch officer, yet he has his face in every situation. He's Exec—executive officer, second in command. In truth there would be few any better for the job. And if pressed, Chief would agree with me. The two long ago found a way past their contempt for each other. Chief lets Hagemann go about his blustery ways and, in the end, he ignores him and does what he wants.

Chief's got his father's haughtiness in him. It's a wonder he trained for anything other than commander. Even so he never fails me. He's the one maneuvering the boat in whatever situation God and the Tommies throw our way, and secretly he likes nothing better than a crisis only he has an answer for. At those times the U-boat is in his hands more than mine. Yet when the day is done, it is still me he answers to. Something he resents to his core in all likelihood, though he knows better than to ever show it.

One sinking to our credit. There would be no prolonged revelry. Lorient is a long way off and there will be more days to celebrate. A reasonable start, no more.

A U-boat patrol requires every fraction of every man, and it's a fool of a captain who thinks there will not be a loose nut or two to keep in place. Forging harmony with the next fellow, that above all is what's needed of a crew. We're die-hard brothers, and there's no room for contrariness getting in the way of the job. I'll tolerate it at the meal table, but I won't if there are depth charges ringing in our ears. There isn't one of them who would dare defy me on that point.

There's not a man aboard who wouldn't stretch himself to that last millimeter. Afterwards, when it is over and we've come through, I make sure he knows I know it, and everyone around him. U-69 is a cigar tube of forty-seven men, breathing the air that everyone else is breathing, eating food that only gets more rank and monotonous with every day that passes, shitting where someone else shit ten seconds before.

I keep a private journal of the men, each name heading a separate page. I call it The History Book. On occasion I add a simple pencil sketch, if the man's face prompts it.

I've noted their birthplace, something of their families, their training, and then incidents, aboard the U-boat or off, worthy of remembering. In some cases minor, but all of importance in painting a picture of the man, whether the lowest ranking seamen or the officers who share the control room. Hagemann has blossomed to a second page. Umbeck has a solid half. And as for Schieder, I've yet to crack the man beyond a sentence or two. He plays by the rule book and there is no need repeating what that book already makes amply clear.

'Know your men.' If there is anything I took from Wolfgang Lüth, this is it. The Nazis hold him up as the man to run a U-boat, with the tonnage to prove it. I encountered him in Kiel. Make each of your men part of something bigger than his function, let them up the conning tower one by one and out into the fresh air when you can. It's not a man and his job. You're on a mission together.

All shrewd insight. Not that I would take everything the man preaches at his word. To my mind he can be altogether too starched. He allows his men little life beyond his rules—no music of their own choosing, nothing other than what he has authorized, no pictures of women that make crewmen feel like men, no smoking before breakfast. From what others have told me, the books they bring aboard must first pass through his hands. To the Reich he is a hero. Twenty-seven ships sunk by last count, and still going strong. Who can argue?

No doubt Lüth would not tolerate loose talk around the officers' table. I have my limits, which the men know well enough, but I can enjoy a good taunting as much as the next fellow. I take a man with all his foibles and deal with him as a man, not as someone to manipulate for my convenience. There is never a doubt who has the last word.

With the first sinking came the satisfaction of having it out of the way, no more thought of returning to port with zero marking the tally sheet. There is always that possibility. It goes without saying the days of brilliant tallies are past. Gone are the patrols when Lüth could sink four ships of 35,000 GRT in one night's hunt. His medals must weigh him down.

Our Metox never failed us, but the detection equipment of the escorts and the air patrols were a running nuisance, sending us constantly to the cellar. We left the St. Lawrence River and went back into the Gulf. There we had more breathing room. A few searchlights on land, but nothing to worry us. No radar signals that weren't diminished by a change of course. In daylight we pressed on at periscope depth, then cruised the surface at night.

In the early hours of the 13th came a radio message from headquarters—three grain carriers, *Formosa, Camelia,* and *Eros,* heading toward us, likely destination Montreal. We are given orders to cruise back and forth between the North Cape of Cape Breton and St. Paul Island. Grid BB 54.

Our nerves stiff at the thought. Eels locked in their firing tubes. Hagemann and the torpedo men rigid with readiness. The first watch officer was steel-faced, in desperate need of discharging energy. In the control room there is no room for it.

'Have a look.'

He took the periscope position I had just vacated.

'What is it?' Though I knew already.

He took a moment. 'Swedes,' he said. 'Idiots!'

Not such idiots. Their flags were perfectly visible. We are under strict orders not to touch the neutral Swedes.

Hagemann stood to one side and exhaled loudly. I motioned to Umbeck to have his look. Umbeck took a few seconds and drew back quickly.

He turned to me. 'Nothing more to be done, *Oberleutnant zur See*.'

Hagemann eyed the second watch officer, taking a dim view of his formal tone.

'They would have made an excellent addition.' I tried not to tally the GRT.

'Headquarters would not be amused.' Umbeck smiled in resignation.

There was, after all, no point getting ourselves in a snarl over it.

'Idiots,' Hagemann said again.

'They have their logic,' said Umbeck, who by then should have known better than to contradict his senior watch officer.

'Fucking pig-shit idiots.'

Umbeck finally took the point, and Hagemann quit the room without looking my way.

Two entries for the The History Book, although neither was particularly deserving. Still, they would add colour to the pages. I wondered what Lüth's reaction would have been.

There was nothing to do but wander about in search of more honest game. I was feeling in a defiant mood and thinking music would ease the work of returning the torpedoes to their racks. Until that was done there was little sleep to be had. The bow torpedo compartment is where half the crew have their bunks.

I passed word to the radioman and when he had readied the gramophone I retrieved the record from my sleeping quarters and handed it to him.

'Something new, Captain. The men are sure to appreciate something new.' Hebestreit enjoyed the covertness of it, the fact that only the two of us had any inkling that the ship would suddenly awake from its disappointment with some melodic surprise.

Hebestreit hadn't bothered to read the label, had likely assumed Liszt or perhaps a sprightly operetta. He was not prepared for trombone and trumpet. A few seconds after the first strains he emerged from his cubbyhole. 'Captain?'

I drew back the curtain from where I lay across the bed. 'Is something the matter, *Oberfunkmaat?*'

'Did you make a mistake, Captain?'

'What mistake?'

'The music, sir. Jazz, sir.'

'Yes, jazz.'

At that moment, Umbeck appeared, more alert than I had seen him since he first boarded the U-boat.

'*Oberleutnant* Gräf.'

'Yes, *Leutnant*.'

'Is it…is it the correct selection?'

'*It Don't Mean A Thing, If It Ain't Got that Swing*.' My pronunciation lacked precision, although it retained a good rhythm.

They both retreated, their uneasiness only marginally diminished. 'You do not like jazz?'

'I was told,' Umbeck said, 'in *Marineakademie*…'

Hebestreit slipped back to his cubbyhole and donned his headphones. Umbeck followed me to the bow compartment. I reached my hand ahead to open the circular hatch.

One of the torpedoes was just being hoisted back into its place on the racks. Slowly, very carefully. Except among the men guiding the operation, a clownish, swing-time atmosphere churned through the room. One fellow, his back to me, was flailing about, impersonating the singer.

A few seconds after my head appeared everyone stood dead still, all but those moving the eel. 'Continue, gentlemen.' I smiled and withdrew my head. 'In you go, Umbeck. Enjoy yourself while you can.'

'*Jawohl*, Captain,' he said sheepishly. I waited until he had wormed his way through. I drew the hatch closed.

If I were to write a rule book for U-boat operations, I would say shake the men up now and then, give them something unexpected to stir their blood. Lüth said to me he would no more have American jazz aboard his boat than he would a Jew. Of course the *Kriegsmarine* forbids both. Who am I to defy Lüth and his cherished conformity.

Lundrigan has taken to the leather divan that stretches along one wall of the lounge. Bride fitted him out with a pillow and blankets. It is not the best solution, but it'll have to do. Regardless, he wouldn't be one to complain.

There's just Bride and John left at the table. John is brooding.

She tells him London is full of sweet young things looking for excitement.

He smiles a broken, solitary smile, his voice muted so it doesn't bother Lundrigan. He promises Bride he'll send her a letter from England, with his picture. In his uniform.

She's got to love him. And she's got to prepare for her heart to be broken if ever anything should happen to him. She wonders what his parents will say about it all.

She learns for the first time there was only ever his mother, that John's father was killed in the First War, a man he had never known. Even so, he's not lamenting it. He's had his whole life to deal with the consequences.

They are about to call it a night when into the lounge slink Hank and Buzz. A pair of lost sheep.

Hank is wondering if they might stretch out in the lounge for the night. There's not much starch left in the G.I.

He's none too pleased with his sailor friend. Buzz gave up their cabin to a woman and her children who had been left sitting up all night. She was desperate, according to Buzz. Hank scoffs.

And as for Charlotte, she is sound asleep by now. Martha was happy enough to see her, finally. Martha shut their cabin door in Hank's face.

John can't resist embracing the turn of events. He offers to get them each a drink. 'A drink,' he proposes, 'to drown sorrows.' His big Texan sorrows.

It's obvious to Bride where this is going, and she knows it's no place good. Buzz has made his way to the piano. He starts to play "I'll Be Seeing You."

For the moment Bride gives into it. 'In all the old familiar places…'

She stops abruptly. She prods John into heading off to his cabin. She directs the other two to where they will find blankets and pillows, suddenly emphatic that they all need their sleep. Another few hours and the ferry will be preparing to dock.

The *Caribou* is nearing its quietest hour.

Before it stirs again in anticipation of setting ashore in Newfoundland. There is little more than the thick breathing of its engines to mark the time. The ship has drawn into itself, set aside its human measure, leaving the hard-hewn grace of steel and science to carry on the journey home.

My last log entry for the 13th of October. At 2357 German Legal Time, U-boat 69 breaks the surface of the Cabot Strait. Proceeding at cruising speed back and forth, course of 295 degrees and 115 degrees respectively.

A U-boat is at its artful best in darkness. Lurking about the pitch, gently slicing seawater undetected. It can bring an abrupt smile to a commander's face. There is nothing that suits me better than standing on the bridge, enfolded in darkness, whether in the face of wind or driving snow, or in these dead hours before any hint of day.

14.10.1942

0000 Grid BB 5459

0400 Grid BB 5464

0534 Grid BB 5456

Wind light from the west, sea state—calm, cloud cover—0.1, barometer—1026 mb, very good visibility, faint northern lights.

When the bridge watch changes in the middle of the night, neither crew is surprised to see me. The new watch settles in and I take a position in the centre of the men. Zeiss issue to his eyes, each man slowly sweeps his quadrant, his ninety degrees of the horizon line. Sure and steady, then at intervals a quick respite of the weighty glasses, a momentary rest for his eyes and arms, before returning the binoculars to begin again.

I am not there to test their competence, or assert my authority, rather to emphasize that point of connection, the link between us all. Their eyes are the eyes of the U-boat, their triumph of discovery crucial to the survival of every man aboard. They each know that—Hagemann, Ehrlich, Langhof, Wimmer. The first watch officer would have drilled it into the other three within a fraction of their lives. Yet I like to think there is something the presence of the captain brings to the mood of the night patrol.

Wimmer is the youngest, the one most thickly dressed. He hasn't yet had to endure true cold, cold that turns saltwater spray on a sou'wester to a sheeting of ice. He can be forgiven. He will know it soon enough, God willing. For now a heavy sweater under his leather coat, woolen scarf and woolen hat. Leather gloves to grip the cold metal casing of the binoculars. He sets himself rigidly in place.

'*Bootsmaat* Wimmer.'

'*Oberleutnant* Gräf.'

'Tell me, Wimmer, how is Bremen faring in the war.' If he is surprised that I remember his home city, it is not obvious. There is the barest of shutters in the progression of the binoculars from left to right.

'The bombing, sir, my father, sir… My mother has moved in with my uncle.'

'I am sorry to hear it, Wimmer.'

'*Atlas Werk* lost some buildings, sir, but I suspect it has recovered.'

'Your mother?'

'She would have preferred I stayed ashore.'

'As they all would.'

'Yes, sir.'

My time on the bridge passes without anything out of the ordinary. Most watches are that—tedious business which grows more tedious as the hours pass. On this night the moonlight at least defines the horizon. There is more than blackness to tire the eyes. I have my stretch at it to give each of them a reprieve, a cigarette if they wish it. And then, before retiring below, I take the moment to let the night silence surround me. To breathe it in. The anticipation offers the finest moment. There is nothing to compare with that first spotting, the moment when the inkling turns into the enemy ship, forming itself into a possibility. It reminds me of an unknown woman revealing herself through fog on a deserted street, her hand tight to the collar of her trench coat, her figure impossibly smart.

Bride slips along the passageway to her cabin. She is singing quietly to herself as she disappears. *I'll be seeing you, in all the old familiar places.* John turns to listen, as her voice fades perfectly away. He loves hearing her sing when she thinks no one is listening. Her voice leaves a trail and he catches its final, barest fragment as he descends to his own cabin.

A few minutes later he's back up again, now at the railing, peering into the near black of night.

He questions whether his eyes are as keen as his father's, those of a sniper, the sharpest in the regiment if he is to believe the stories. His father had an eye for Turks. And would have had an eye for Germans had he not been killed.

John has in his hand the scope Sam gave him, the one used in the Gallipoli trenches. Sam was the spotter; his father pulled the trigger. John steadies the scope against an upright and trains it on the horizon line, moving slowly, deliberately across a portion of the line. It is more strongly defined than on the other nights he has done it. There is moonlight to thank for that.

He imagines what might trace itself within that line, though his expectation is that nothing will. Nothing capable of bending his mind from the *Caribou* cutting its path across the Strait. Yet a scope is in need of a target, a piece of enemy to taunt and threaten with the pulling of a trigger.

Never has he felt closer to his father. Never has he sensed him more, his father's breathing touching his neck, his words guiding what to be looking for, his father's heart in tandem with his own. John has often thought of what it was for his father to spend day after day with a rifle to his eye, in need of someone to kill.

If a U-boat were to show itself, what luck that would be. John would have his wish, the crosshairs bearing the shaft of a torpedo ready to spring, him sounding the alarm for the ferry to make its escape, the escort to attack.

The instrument eventually falls away, unfulfilled. And there is just the night, as before. He hesitates for a moment. Then thinks no more about it. He returns the scope to its moleskin sleeve, retreats inside, and descends the stairs to his room.

The words of the song linger. Like the last notes on the piano, they fade to a thin echo. They slip with Bride into her cabin.

She drops onto the bed and quickly releases her feet from her shoes. She stretches her legs out in front of her and leans back. The relief is immense, as if an inordinately tight bandage had been cut free. She sighs theatrically.

Age, she admits. Every night—as she massages her ankles and the portion of each foot she can reach—she wonders how many more years she can keep it up. Yet, come morning, she will be as eager as the girl who shipped out from Bay Roberts so many years before.

She manages to change into a loose-fitting nightgown, before falling into bed. Her lifebelt is within reach, though she has not given it any thought. Her prayers bear the greater trust. A few words after the 'Our Father,' as on every night. Lord, keep us safe.

I'll find you in the morning sun…and when the night is new…

All is quiet, Harold reports.

Taverner tells Harold to catch a couple of hours of sleep while he can.

His son returns the advice, before heading off.

Taverner nods. Into the dark he wishes him good night.

The captain is on deck alone. On the bridge, Jim Prosper, Second Officer, is in charge, crewman Jack Dominie at the wheel, and two more men on watch duty. The vessel is on its final stretch to port.

Before long, Millie will stir, early as she always is, out of bed before anyone else in the house, awaiting her husband and her pair of sons. She'll sit at the kitchen table in her tartan flannel robe, its corded belt tied loosely around her waist. She'll sit in the dark with tea in her favourite cup, looking out the window, watching the slow transformation to daylight.

Taverner turns away from the same unknown night, and takes to his cabin, thinking on the day ahead. It is close enough that when he lies across the bed he remains fully dressed. He has only to rise up and step outside when the time comes, with the lighthouse at Channel Head once more in perfect view.

THE CURTAIN DOES NOTHING TO ISOLATE ME FROM THE ambivalence of life aboard a U-boat. Whatever prize a patrol delivers, uncertainty follows. A misstep away from catastrophe, an equal step from glory.

I breathe and a tangle of breaths are meters away. Except for the four men on the bridge, a pair in the engine room, another in the control room, the crew is fitfully dormant.

Even so they are raw with conviction, fixed to a life as few ever are. In the fog of my half-sleep, half-faith, there is a lull. I know it in the cadence within my chest, slowed to something resembling stoicism. Life goes on.

Then, at its most restful, sudden uproar from the control room.

'Commander to the bridge! Black smoke!'

I am on my feet in an instant, grabbing the binoculars. Into the control room, a scramble to the conning tower and the bridge.

'Show me.' I turn to the quadrant where Exec's binoculars are trained.

'Forty degrees,' Hagemann pronounces.

A trail of soot visible to the naked eye. The view through the binoculars verifies its source. A shadow of a steamer belching black against the murkiness of a moon-faint sky. I fix to it. A freight and passenger steamer? Behind it a second shadow. An escort without doubt.

'What do you make of it, Captain?'

Make of it?

A steamer in total blackout. There is only one thing to make of such a vessel. The ferry crossing the Strait. On its route to Newfoundland.

Make of it?

A target, there can be no doubt. Military aboard, as we know from intelligence.

Civilians as well. The other steadfast conclusion. The briefest pause, an intake of air.

That is the price. The dealings of war. Ask the dead of Cologne, of Hamburg. Ask Wimmer about the dead of Bremen.

'Maneuver ahead.'

'Yes, Captain.'

'Tube five.'

Exec is surprised. My decision is to fire from the single stern torpedo tube, not any of the four tubes in the bow. 'One eel, sir?'

'I trust your aim, Hagemann.'

He looks at me with a quick, unflinching smile.

'Action stations!' My words flash through the ship.

The U-boat comes alive.

Men drop from their bunks in fractured unison, like the bullet release of bodies at a road race. A scramble to dress, to stow away the remnants of night. An instant queue to the latrine.

A vehement mutter. 'Quick, you laggards! There's a war on, or don't you know it!'

Hagemann calls from the bridge 'Tube five!' The words repeated, doubling over themselves, an echo stretching to both ends of the boat. 'Tube five! Tube five!' The return version as loud as the first.

Their call to arms. In the aft-most compartment, the torpedo men take charge, clearing access to the tube where the eel has been lying in wait, ready for the firing line between the twin rudders. Here also are the electric motors, dormant until the U-boat dives. For now the engineers are in the adjacent compartment, attending the diesels.

There is no slowing the urgency. It is not in their training, even though it will take time to get the U-boat in position, a while of creeping in increments through the black of night.

In due time, up from the bowels of the ship, 'Tube five, ready!'

On the bridge Exec is consumed by the precision needed to plant U-69 in the best position. He orders the *Überwasserzieloptik* fixed to its pedestal. He plants his eyes against its binoculars, adjusting steadily, steadily, until the prize lies through the cross-hairs of the UZO.

'Range?'

'1800 meters.'

We need to be closer, at least by half. But I say nothing to Hagemann. He's in his glory.

I'm locked onto my own binoculars. I would have thought the escort would be circling the ferry. Instead, it trails obediently aft. With each passing minute I grow more and more confident that neither ship has any suspicion we are so close. Both claiming a steady, unencumbered passage home. Landfall near enough to taste.

'Target speed and course?' Hagemann calls to the navigator in the control room.

'Enemy speed 10.5 knots. Course forty degrees,' reports Janssen.

Exec and the navigator must work like twins if we are to make the kill. Janssen is a year older than I am, another three older than

Hagemann. He has the brains and patience of any man aboard. Hagemann appreciates the fact.

I give Exec all the time he needs. By 0800, U-69 is on the verge of its crucial position.

'Range?'

'Six-five-zero.'

'Target bow right, bearing nine-zero, target speed one-two knots.'

'Open tube door!'

A few seconds later, the comeback, 'Tube five flooded!'

'Stand by!' yells Hagemann. He awaits the final order from me.

My gloved hands are like iron clenching the binoculars. My heart pumps madly. A hungry missile to unleash, frantic to send the enemy into chaos.

It is neither right nor wrong. It is what I am here to do, a U-boat commander, every particle drilled to within that fraction of a second.

In wait, nerves pitched to the edge of the verdict. In desperate need of relief.

'Permission to fire!'

Hagemann, bent into the eyepieces, right hand on the firing lever, must take it to its absolute end.

'Connect tube five!' he barks. It echoes through the ship.

Another echo returns. 'Tube five ready to fire!'

'Tube five…' At that second Hagemann jerks the lever. 'Fire!'

A hulking, willful jolt.

The torpedo lunges from the ship, severing black water, locked on the enemy that trails black, indecent smoke.

THE PASSENGER FERRY LIES TWENTY MILES OFF CHANNEL Head. At the moment, Taverner is fixed upright in the pitch black of the cabin.

The *Caribou* moves in innocence, only the abiding rhythm of its engines, performing perfectly, seeking home.

Through the quiet comes a faint call from the sea, a pulse, a reticent surge growing minutely louder. It calls Taverner to the deck, to where he stands alone, looking across the waters, wondering who might be looking back at him.

When the bullet strikes, there is no surprise.

A savage thrust, one boat to another.

It jolts him to his knees.

'*Oberleutnant!*'

Hagemann's avowal of victory. Before my bare eyes the torpedo strikes amidships, exploding skyward, a vehement flare of smoke and fire.

'*Oberleutnant*!'

The next second, another explosion, gouging deeper into the hull. The boiler blowing apart, fuming steam. Seawater floods in.

The ship begins its death tilt to port.

I smile at Hagemann, the old reliable. For a second only, for we are supremely vigilant, binoculars locked now on the escort vessel.

'Range?'

'Nine-five-zero.'

'Position?'

'Ten degrees forward.'

The escort wheels first toward the crippled ship. For the first time I see passengers at the ferry's railing.

The escort spots us and cuts in our direction. The rush to ram us is on.

'Alarm!'

Everyone swarms to the hatch, grabs the rail, and drops down the hole like clockwork. Wimmer, Ehrlich, Langhof, Hagemann. I scramble behind Exec. Stall a few steps down the ladder to pull shut the hatch cover, wrenching the hand wheel to lock it in place.

The exhaust and air intake ducts are shut. The diesels stopped, the E-motors geared into the drive shafts.

'Vents clear!' bellows Chief.

'Flood!' I shout out a half-second later.

The air in the buoyancy tanks thunders from the ship. Seawater rushes in.

'Forward plane, hard down.'

'Aft plane, ten down.'

U-69 plunges, bow first. Every expendable crewman rushes forward for the extra weight.

Suddenly all is silence, except for the muffled hum of the E-motors. Eyes are fixed on the depth gauge. Its needle sinks—twenty meters, fifty, 100, down, down. Everyone grips something to keep himself vertical. Chief begins to right the boat.

The word reaches us. 'Balanced!'

We have levelled out.

In that instant Bride is a dazed heap on the cabin floor, clenched in the pain that pounds at her knee.

She struggles to her feet. Her shoes have slid to a wall. In the effort to reach them she falls again, inflicting another surge of pain.

Suddenly everything is black.

Bride sweeps her hands about the floor and manages to gather up her shoes. She drags herself to the bed, sits upright along its edge, enough to force her feet into them.

She cripples in the direction of the cabin door. It's too late when she remembers her lifebelt. She'll never find it now.

Outside, the ship is hell.

Lt. James Cuthbert blares into the night a second time.

The first tremor was unmistakable. The second marks death.

From the deck of the escort vessel, he sights the *Caribou* gutted amidships, already listing. The sounds of the pandemonium faint at this distance, amplified a thousand times over in his head.

The hunt for the U-boat is on. A half-dozen binoculars scan the direction from which the torpedo fired. There, on the surface still, as if reveling in what it has done.

Cuthbert's orders set a new course for *Grandmère*, but the time it takes is agonizing, made worse by the chaos through the binoculars when he turns them again toward the ferry. He has no choice. The navy's orders are to attack the enemy. Destroy it at all costs.

He bellows for depth charges.

Confirmation comes instantly from the aft deck, the launchers already poised to shed their loads.

He can tell the U-boat captain knows what's to follow. Its bow sunk below the surface, its stern following, slippery as an eel. The sea has swallowed it.

Screams of desperation hurl from all parts of the ship.

In his rush to help, John discovers Bride barely upright at the railing, both hands clasped fiercely to it.

He is frantic to overpower the chaos. He frees himself of his lifebelt and forces it onto her, tightening it as much as his fumbling hands can manage.

Her head jolts wildly. She yells past him into the darkness, yells for passengers to find their lifeboat stations.

The stairwell is bedlam. Seawater curls about passengers fighting their way through it from the cabins below.

She orders John away from her. The children, help the children.

Two of the lifeboats on the starboard side have been blasted to shreds. Only the aft boat remains.

The Strickland family have dragged themselves from below deck, the mother clutching the baby, the father clutching the older girl. John hurriedly leads them aft, the walk an erratic, angled clamber along the railing. The ship lists deeper and deeper to port. The bow has given in, set to slide beneath the waves.

When they reach the lifeboat, it is in the water, tossing madly about, another four passengers aboard and gripping the gunwales for their lives. With her husband's help, Gertie Strickland lowers herself and the baby into the boat, where she sits, young Nora clenched to her, peering desperately back up at her husband. William pulls the older girl, Abigail, away from him and hangs her above the boat, her arms and legs flailing wildly. No sooner has he dropped her into the waiting arms of his wife than he jumps himself. At that moment a manic wave smacks the lifeboat against the ship, capsizing it, pitching everyone into the sea.

The parents scream for their children. The older girl is nowhere to be seen. The sea has seized her, and now turns to the others. The father's right hand grasps the baby's nightgown, holding the child's head above the water, a cold, sodden bundle, more dead than alive. John braces himself with one hand against the railing, leans over to his limit, far enough that he can snatch the child. Someone behind him claims her, freeing him to do what he can to help the father and then his wife latch onto the railing and drag themselves over it, back onto the ship.

The railing has leaned further, now near level with the ocean. The *Caribou* is not long for anything but the ocean floor.

The sea-battered couple cling to each other, their piteous baby wedged between, two lifebelts woefully unfit.

John coils about, desperate to find hope that anything can be done. The water has reached their knees, washing higher. The nightmare tract of grey-black sea swells in deference to mercy. If the band of humans holds out long enough, the sea will set them afloat. Or drown them. The suction of a sinking vessel waits, prepared to drag them under, no one to break the surface alive.

John screams that they must get away from the ship. It's their only chance.

To purge their hopes, a wall of ocean breaks over the railing, over the cluster of terrified souls, sending each of them to their own solitary fight for breath. The Strickland baby swirls past his eyes and into the blackness, no chance of a saviour.

John knows how to swim, enough to battle for a stroke that will keep his head above water. He knows frigid flesh, as a teenage boy chasing about icebergs with Dr. Grenfell. It is the Doctor's unflinching voice that prods him on, stroke by stroke, to drive himself from the ship.

When he glances back, the *Caribou* is gone, but for the naked curl of propeller, what should never know air. And suddenly it shamefully follows what remains of the ship into the enfolding depths of the sea.

Bride clings to the railing iron, as if the strength of iron were her strength. Stronger still is the ocean, the infinite fluid that filled the decks below, that usurped the air, the same that laps at the iron, swamping about her ankles, and now her knees.

She calls to Him. Sweet, sweet Jesus.

As if she had embraced Him all her life, had not ignored Him until He is her only hope of deliverance.

The children. Help the poor children.

The torment of the living washes over her, her soul lashed against the railing iron.

In the sweet by and by, we shall meet on that beautiful shore...

Her voice is mute, like the frantic cries now swallowed within the ship, leaving only those that rend the rising sea, that slash vainly against its enormity.

In the sweet by and by. In the sweet by and by...

The shore washes over her.

A just life should bring a just end. A man abides each hour in such faith. But war cares nothing for saneness and robs Taverner of a rightful death.

He helped what few passengers he could, now wills himself to the deck railing for what he knows must be the final seconds, casting behind him the futile hope of doing anything more. Stanley and Harold seek him out, one after the other. He grips their hands and sends them on their way. Duty outweighs the burden of family.

Harold hesitates, returning to stand with his father.

Harold's voice defies the mayhem—the captain has done all that can be done.

His son. His mother needs him.

They stand silently, their hands gripping the rail. The stern rises steadily, the sea swells over the bow. It circles before them.

Harold curses it savagely. Taverner moves his hand to encase his son's. The grip holds for the second until his father releases him and Harold is gone.

The captain claims the memory of his wife. Stay safe. The family is in her hands.

The *Caribou* descends head-first to meet the sea.

There is no sight of land, no sight of Germans. But they are for certain there, their duty done.

The *Caribou,* her balance impossibly askew, surrenders to the sea. Filling the air—the final strains of a miserable chorus, a fading pitch of barren cries that cease one by one, with the vessel falling methodically beneath the swell.

Taverner plants his feet and welds himself to the rail. The sea swirls about him, lashing higher and higher and he stands rigid, defying its buoyancy, in the blameless wish to be dragged wherever his ship has the heart to go.

Cuthbert reels, as if struck by the butt of a rifle's recoil.

The *Caribou* has perished, a violent warp of sea left in her wake.

The surface is sorely restless. One lifeboat, perhaps another, several navy rafts. A ghastly scattering of survivors. The darkness denies him clear sight of them.

But there is no escaping their pleas. The strongest pierce the darkness and lodge within him, a current through his heart, through his limbs, steeling his grip on the binoculars that sweep back to where the U-boat took its dive. Behind him now a distant murmur, a morbid psalm at his back.

There is no time to dwell on it. Not now, not with the taunting swirl of water where the U-boat dove.

It's his only gauge for the depth charges. He sets a triangular pattern for six of them a short distance beyond the wake.

Now! And now!

Reposition—then two more. Reposition—two more again.

The escort waits, until 150 feet below the surface comes the jolt of the explosions. With any luck on Cuthbert's part, a death stroke among them.

Luck. What is it but guesswork? The ASDIC shows nothing, a useless piece of equipment at this range.

His only choice is to make a grid and follow it, quadrant by quadrant. The incessant ping of the ASDIC detects nothing still. The depth charges are throwing it off, making it even more useless than before.

Like their asdic—impotent. Its range—hopeless. Hagemann, by how many meters have we escaped? By my calculation, more than enough to breathe easy. If never entirely easy, for war is as much chance below the water as it is above. The Canadians can get as lucky as the rest.

I need not worry. Listen. It is not depth charges that make such a sound. Hear it? The ferry buckling beneath the pressure of its depth. Hear it? The crush of her hull, the tearing apart of her bulkheads. The opera of the macabre. The cacophony of war.

I would escape it if I could, if it did not serve a purpose. The captain of a u-boat must be a clever man. I will turn u-69 toward this resonance, not away.

This for the log: u-69 is settling near the sunken ship. The Canadian will not come here to fire his depth charges for fear of striking the lifeboats. Afloat above us are those who escaped the ferry before she sank, clinging to life, oblivious to what lies beneath them. They are not far from land. In daylight will come their rescuers. But for now they are my shield.

Do they not call us *wolf*—the most cunning of their animals? Do they think we will not live up to the name?

The chaos enveloped him, with only instinct to plough a way through it, no time to figure if it could have been different. There is not a man who steps onto a gangplank that doesn't wonder what he'll do if the rig he's standing on goes under.

When the torpedo struck, Alex was on deck, forward on the starboard side, having a last smoke, his hand covering the cigarette. The steward was just about to take to his bunk for the night when it hit, not twenty yards from where he was standing. It slammed him to the deck. He crawled to his feet. The boilers blew, decimating the engine room and its crew, sending a massive shudder through the ship.

Alex could find no trace of the two starboard lifeboats. He rushed to the port side, yelling at everyone he encountered to do the same. There he discovered dozens jammed aboard a lifeboat, refusing to get out so the boat could be lowered into the sea. The crewmen had no choice but to climb aboard and cut it from the davits. The lifeboat struck the ocean with a thunderous smack and immediately started to fill with seawater.

Alex knew right away what was wrong. He wedged himself among the dumbfounded lot until he found the bilge hole and the plug chained next to it. Every time he tried to jam it in, the force of the water blew it out again. The lifeboat capsized, throwing everyone into the sea. The whole lot of them were yelling and screaming, nothing but pandemonium. The strongest hauled themselves on top of the overturned boat, only to be pitched back into the sea again.

Alex doesn't know how much time has passed. He's in the water, others not far off, with nothing he can do to help them. He is barely able to help himself. He doesn't have a lifebelt. He can't swim, but he happens upon a scrap of plank big enough to keep him afloat. He wonders if it is wood from one of the lifeboats smashed to pieces when the torpedo struck.

The man knows nothing but to doggedly heed the compulsion to survive. He clenches the wood, sluggishly flailing about in waterlogged clothes, somehow keeping his head above water.

He kicks with whatever energy he can summon to drive himself away from the undertow caused by the sinking ship. The plank is useless for more than one man. Others are left to wrestle with the water, every man for himself, every woman and child.

After endless minutes he catches sight of a lifeboat. He kicks with whatever is left in him. He closes in enough to recognize the one person aboard. Lundrigan. The fellow is bailing as fast as he can, but Alex knows what is wrong. The plug is out of her. Find the damn plug. Lundrigan looks up, too afraid to stop what he's doing.

Lundrigan nods to Alex and the others. He is holding up, despite his heart. He's managed to stay drier than the others who made it to the lifeboat. He's the great exception.

It was a desperate struggle to get Alex aboard, the whole time trying to keep the boat from swamping. But together they managed it. They got to the plug, wedged it in and kept it in. They saved themselves, then saved whoever else was in reach and alive.

An inconsolable Mrs. Shiers sits next to Lundrigan, his overcoat bundled around her to keep out the cold. She's all the time crying because she and her boy were flung apart in the chaos. Sitting on the bottom of the boat is the nurse Charlotte, in mute shock still about what became of her friend, and John, lying in the bow, the torn sleeve of a shirt as a makeshift bandage around his thigh.

Having come through it, they're overwhelmed, each in their own way.

Despite his pain, John rages at the fact the plugs had been left out of the lifeboats. He curses the man who issued the regulation.

Mrs. Shiers has no mind for it. She pleads for him to stop. It is not what the good Lord wants of them, not if her son is to be saved.

'The boy is fine.' Lundrigan has no way of knowing this, but that doesn't stop him. He's sure someone would have seen young Leonard and hauled him from the water.

John is far from sure. But he holds back about the Strickland children.

Leonard is fifteen months old and all he is wearing is a white flannel nightshirt made by his grandmother. His mother knows the chance of his survival is poor. Unless her prayers have been answered, unless someone came upon him in a lifeboat or raft and was able to get him aboard. Even then, it's likely he would have been too cold and drained of life to make it through.

No one aboard the boat truly believes there's a chance the child is alive. But Lundrigan, the stanch Salvationist, is not about to let Mrs. Shiers sink into despair.

John is certain no miracle saved Miss Fitzpatrick. She had his lifebelt but it was never tightened properly and he knows for a fact she couldn't swim. Whatever the case, the lifebelt wasn't going to save a woman of her size. Alex peers at John and shakes his head.

John will only ever admire her, will always think of Bride as a good woman who should never have drowned.

And Captain Ben. Alex saw him right after it happened. He saw there was nothing Taverner could do, any more than any of the crew. All around them was madness. Taverner had helped what passengers he could aboard lifeboats, but could do nothing much in the five minutes they had. He was struggling back to the bow of the ship. That was the last Alex saw of him.

Taverner had been wound taut before the *Caribou* was struck, like no one had ever seen him before, like he was fighting against himself to keep it inside.

Hank wasn't sure he had it in him to see daylight again.

But as he was schooled to do, he put his faith in God, who has His ways, as Hank had always been told. And sure enough, a lifebelt appeared, floating not ten strokes away from where Hank broke the surface. Uncle Sam had made sure Hank knew how to swim, and the good Lord did the rest. As Hank's father liked to say, the two together make for a powerful team. One you always want on your side.

His friend Buzz had not fared as well. Before they jumped together into the sea, Buzz had yelled back. Yes, he could swim. But when Hank finally cleared his head above the water and caught his breath, he called and called to his friend, one of dozens of exhausted voices skimming the surface of the sea. Nothing came back. It tore at his guts to think the sea had hauled Buzz under and worn him out.

To Lundrigan, there is always hope. To Lundrigan, you are born with hope and if you die, you die with it.

Hank had held on to hope, and then he had heard voices close to him. He'd strained his ears to their limit, all the while his eyes burning with saltwater and darkness.

He'd given it every ounce of lung power left in him. And when someone aboard the lifeboat finally answered, it was as if heaven had opened up and said the world needed him awhile longer.

'Thanks be to Jesus. Thanks be to Jesus.'

Lundrigan had seen Hank and Buzz lose their fight with the suction when the ship went under. He had figured they were both goners.

But Hank reached the lifeboat, and with Lundrigan to one side and Alex on the other, he was heaved over the gunwale and dragged aboard.

One almighty catch they hadn't counted on, according to Alex.

There was just enough energy left in Hank for him to kiss the dog tags and the St. Christopher medal that hung together around his neck.

There's a moment for Buzz, but when Hank's eyes clear enough to see into the gloom surrounding him, he's cut short.

It's John all right. Roughed up, but alive. The lifeboat came back on him when he was trying to get aboard. When he did manage it he discovered in all the turmoil his leg had been sliced open. He's lost a lot of blood.

Hank notices Mrs. Shiers for the first time. She mumbles about the boy.

He shakes his head. Though he had heard a child crying, perhaps more than one. Mrs. Shiers shrinks back into the coat and draws it tighter.

There's one person Hank has yet to recognize. She's stiff in her wet clothes, bent forward, her head pressed against her knees, her fingers laced through the hair plastered to her head. She rocks herself slightly and stops.

When she speaks, her words crumble. She needs to find Martha. Hank stares in disbelief.

Lundrigan urges her to have faith. It could be that another boat picked up her friend.

Hank reaches out to touch her shoulder. She draws her head tighter to her knees. She's exhausted. She's scared. He calls her name but it startles her.

All she wants is to find Martha.

There's no accounting for who made it and who didn't. Charlotte put every bit of herself into saving Martha, only to watch her drift away from the overturned boat, certain to perish. And Buzz, no sign of him even though he was a good swimmer. Even though a sailor should have had a better chance than most.

Hank survived. As Lundrigan would have it, he deserves to be alive as much as the next fellow.

They all have their families to be thinking about. John has his mother in St. Anthony. Hank has his in Abilene.

For Mrs. Shiers, it's not only Leonard that's on her mind. Or her husband. Mrs. Shiers lays a hand on her stomach, and begins stroking it.

John stiffens. The woman is carrying a baby.

THE FERRY, ITS HULKING FORM PROSTRATE ON THE ocean floor, has lost all purpose, save one. It lies not far below us, soundless, no more a grinding death. It is the U-boat's silent bounty, its comatose protection.

An ill-fit, this huntsman and his prey. The consequences are too close at hand. U-69 should be racing from the scene, leaving the morass to itself, but instead we wait, the dead locked below, the living floating above. It unnerves me.

It's unnerving that I'm grateful there is an escort ship. Someone to turn attention to the survivors. Something I am not about to do.

Last month Dönitz sent new orders, in the days following the sinking of the British troopship *Laconia* by U-156. When the U-boat raised a Red Cross flag and set about to rescue some of the survivors, an American bomber attacked it, even though it had been informed of the mission. Dozens of survivors were killed by the bombs. U-156 barely escaped.

To all Commanding Officers:

1. *No attempt of any kind must be made to rescue members of ships sunk, and this includes picking up persons in the water and putting them in lifeboats, righting capsized lifeboats, and handing over food and water. Rescue runs counter to*

the most elementary demands of warfare for the destruction of enemy ships and crews.

2. *Orders for bringing back captains and chief engineers still apply.*
3. *Rescue the shipwrecked only if their statements will be of importance for your boat.*
4. *Be harsh. Bear in mind that the enemy takes no regard of women and children in his bombing attacks on German cities.*

Tension seeps into every compartment, strokes every crewman with the sharp edge of its fingernails. They wait, and wait, one ear to the outside, the other to the whispered conversations between them. Our dominion is at a standstill. Anxious sweat flows freely.

Oddly, brutishly some would say, it is times like these I come to prize. This ungainly hour when the situation is in our favour, but its outcome far from certain. A situation in need of a tight mind, without second thought.

'Clever stroke, sir,' says Wimmer, lingering in the control room with me, while the navigator is at his charts. Wimmer has no experience to restrain him.

I glance at him, but say nothing. It is a long time to the port of Lorient.

Wimmer is braced with one hand against the iron web, the organized tangle of pipes, ducts, valves, gauges, switches, ventilators, hand wheels. Tight bundles of wires snake through it all.

'We do our best, sir, then it is in God's hands.'

I look up from the *Papenberg* depth gauge, my neck muscles knotted from making calculations in conjunction with the navigator's echo sounder.

'I try not to leave too much to God. He has a great load of men wanting His attention these days.'

It does nothing for him. Wimmer turns silent, conscious of the navigator leaning over his slender table nearby.

No one aboard has a more purposeful job than *Obersteuermann* Janssen. With his protractors, parallel rules, and dividers he's using his charts to plot a route that will speed us away from here. Exactly when we will make the move I've yet to decide. We have the luxury of the hours to when daylight breaks on the survivors.

The strain on the U-boat's batteries is reasonable for the moment, but inevitably we'll be forced to the surface to recharge them. We want to be far away when we do.

'U-69 is not a true submarine.' It is meant for Wimmer. I am not telling him anything he doesn't already know. 'Full out, our batteries last two hours.'

'Yes, sir.'

'Is that all, Wimmer? What if we have no choice and break the surface with the Tommies up our ass?'

He laughs.

'It wasn't meant to amuse you, *Bootsmaat* Wimmer.' My impatience given release, I turn to Janssen and his charts. Wimmer begins to move away. 'Stay, Wimmer. Make yourself useful. Keep an eye on the *Papenberg*.'

'Yes, sir.'

'Wimmer.'

'Yes, sir.'

'The more a U-boatman knows about his ship, the better his chances. Don't be fooled. The Tommies are getting better.'

They are getting very much better, if I am to interpret the radio reports. Since July, U-boat losses have tripled. We are now losing eight to twelve each month. In September there were three commanders from Crew 35 who went to the bottom with their crews. Friedrichs, Lange, and Harney.

I recall Klaus Harney very well from our time on Dänholm. I was nineteen, he had barely turned eighteen, with the face of a twelve year old. Except that he was brilliant (and likely had a father who greased the process), we were all left to wonder how he ever got there. He looked like he should be home in Düsseldorf on his mother's knee. *Korporal* Jodeit made him his personal lackey. Harney survived and by the time we reached officer training the following year he had learned to feign toughness, although he forever looked too boyish and innocent for his uniform. This year the navy boosted him to the rank of *Kapitänleutnant* and sent him off as the first commander of U-756. He was twenty-five. He was dead before he ever sank a ship.

More U-boats are going to the bottom for a single reason. The Tommies and the Yanks have equipped their planes with a new type of radar. There's no denying it any longer. Their laboratories have outsmarted our own. It is only a matter of time before the Canadians have it too.

'Wimmer.'

'Yes, sir.'

'How old are you?'

'Twenty-one.'

'You've done well.'

'There are some nineteen, sir.'

'Every patrol they are getting younger. Why is that, do you think?'

We both know why. He doesn't answer.

'Headquarters has no choice, Wimmer. Soon they will be marching aboard in lederhosen.'

I smile, giving him permission to do the same.
The navigator looks up and catches my eye.

WITH THEIR YOUNG SON, JAMES CUTHBERT AND HIS wife had left Britain and ventured to Canada. For her it was a homecoming. Cuthbert didn't know what to expect.

The Royal Canadian Navy was happy enough to get another career officer. Most of those they have are escorting convoys across the Atlantic, in corvettes and destroyers, ships doing the jobs they were built to do. Not minesweepers, sent off to act as escorts, leaving the Gulf of St. Lawrence a playing field for the Germans.

The HMCS *Grandmère,* in the tradition of the Canadian Navy, was named after a community in Canada. This one in Québec, though there were many in the navy who thought the brass could have settled on something more vigorous than "Grandmother."

Cuthbert decided he'd make do. That, too, he has come to conclude, is in the tradition of the Canadian Navy.

Of the hundred men aboard the *Grandmère* when she went into escort service, only a handful had ever been to sea. It made for a bleak initiation. Yet after three months they had hardened into seamen. Cuthbert is not prone to commendations, but he is well pleased to a man, and, as far as he can tell, they are satisfied to be aboard.

Yet nothing could have prepared them for this.

No notion where the killer has gone. The ASDIC hopeless. A night sea scattered with survivors. Their expectations of rescue distant, fragile. No less chastening.

Cuthbert's constant choice is to return to where the U-boat went under. To illuminate the sea with starshells, to see where to be dropping more depth charges. This time his guess explodes at 500 feet. His goal is for it to further damage a U-boat struck by the first round. He doubts if there is a crewman aboard who would lay a bet on it.

When all his efforts are swallowed by the night, he is left with nothing to do but scour the sea, quadrant by quadrant, with the dimming notion that the U-boat might show itself again.

Emergency kit?

Alex points to the locker beneath the stern thwart. Lundrigan stretches a hand inside and searches about until he retrieves a clammy oilcloth bundle. There's more inside than any of them expected—cans of water and biscuits, four small wool blankets. All recently stocked and dry.

Alex hands Hank a blanket and nods toward Charlotte. He wraps a second around John, careful not to aggravate his wound. With another, Mrs. Shiers covers her legs, which have been shaking constantly.

The three others will take turns with the remaining blanket. Hank searches his pockets and produces a P-38, Army issue can opener. A flat inch and half-piece of metal with a hinged curved blade. A soldier's best friend.

From the emergency kit, Lundrigan retrieves what appears to be the exact same device.

Hank puts his P-38 to work, uncovering the contents of the cans. The drinking water is relief to their salt-crusted lips and parched throats. The food is hard-baked ship's biscuit, with no promise of any taste. Regardless, they dutifully set about eating it.

Suddenly, in the near distance comes the rumble of an underwater explosion. Another depth charge, followed by another round, even stronger.

Just pray they don't come any closer. If it's any comfort, for sure the escort has sent word to Port aux Basques. Fishermen will be out searching for them come daylight.

John is muttering. They could all be frozen to death by daylight. He slumps deeper into the bow of the boat.

Again Mrs. Shiers is on the verge of tears. Charlotte is still lost to herself.

Lundrigan sits silently. He thinks about the others scattered around them in the dark, the dozens fighting as hard as they are to stay alive. How long will the escort keep up the hunt before turning her attention to the survivors? He has no answer. He'll leave it to the Lord, whatever He thinks best.

The man has been a Salvationist all his life. It's taken him through some rough times, although nothing remotely as rough as this. He's decided the ordeal must be telling him something. As they say in the Salvation Army—he's to be a soldier for Christ. That's what it's telling him.

Mrs. Shiers notices his closed eyes, his hands raw with the cold, clasped together. She would like to have a prayer for young Leonard.

Hank is as alert as anyone aboard. She looks at him expectantly. He hesitates.

The words Hank searches for come easily to Lundrigan. With open eyes the Salvationist prays to the Lord to keep young Leonard safe from all harm, to give him strength and courage in the face of all evil.

Mrs. Shiers has had no thought of her young son facing more evil. Cold and water, but not evil.

Amens scatter about the boat, Charlotte's the last.

Lundrigan tells her to rest. The Lord has her friend in His arms.

Mrs. Shiers looks at him. She's sobbing once again.

As much as he wishes otherwise, there's more than prayer on Lundrigan's mind. There are questions nagging him that prayer won't answer. Lundrigan had given up his cabin to Mrs. Shiers and, while she had the worst of it, he was safe enough in the lounge. If it had been him who had to struggle through all that water to get up from below deck his heart might not have stood it. When he jumped into the lifeboat he hardly got wet. Why was he saved?

John, too, has questions. He could have been taken and Miss Fitzpatrick saved, a woman who worked so hard all her life helping people. Or Hank sucked under, and some father saved to see his children again.

And, Leonard?

Perhaps God *is* watching over him.

Mrs. Shiers is not convinced. 'Where was the Lord when the torpedo struck? How could He allow all those children to suffer?'

'If a man loses his faith he has nothing.'

'It is no comfort to a mother when it's her own child who is suffering.'

'There's a war on. The Germans don't give a good goddamn about children.'

'Even their own children? Don't they love them as much as we love ours?'

'Hitler is a savage.'

'What about the man who fired the torpedo? He has a mother and a father who love him, a home to go to after the war is over. What is he thinking?'

We stand motionless and wait. Father, if you were to stand beside me, knowing what this last hour has wrought, what would you think? Above us are the survivors, clinging to life. To a man they are cursing me. Do you hear them, Father? They curse me in the name of the same God you would use to curse the French at Verdun, the same one you use now to curse the English and their planes dropping bombs over our homeland. Can you make sense of it? I am the one who ordered the firing of the torpedo, and I make no sense of it.

What I do grasp is that my actions are bonded to the lives of my men. Every ploy, every maneuver of U-69 is done with them and their families at my back. And yes, you, Father, you are here as well, pressing me on with your silence. I wish I understood more of you, to know what you would think of your son at this very moment.

'Captain.' It is Hebestreit, a welcome relief. He has been listening intently through his hydrophones for the hour since we have gone below. The depth charges have stopped finally, though they have long been out of range.

There is more to report. For the last thirty minutes no more pinging of the escort's ASDIC, nothing to indicate where she sits. It is worse than knowing the ship might be close. Yet, I've every reason to believe she is not. The vessel is not about to wander blindly among the survivors, in the dark more a hazard than a help. And if she were so mindless as to do so, no depth charges would ever leave her decks.

'For all of us a game of waiting, *Oberfunkmaat*.'

'Yes, sir.'

'Shall I play something for the crew? Something to take their minds off it.'

'Beethoven? *Für Elise* perhaps?'

I look at him. 'No.'

He is disappointed. He thought it such a useful suggestion. He likes to be one step ahead of me, in small, insignificant ways. This is not the time.

'Very good, sir.' He retreats stiffly to his nook and dons his hydrophones again.

Elise has been out of my head for several hours and thoughts of her do me no good. Yet the scent of her, the touch of her lips, the brush of my bare skin against hers are all so near me now that for the moment I stand more willfully upright, hand clenched to a pipe overhead, eyes closed.

My heart races, in anticipation of the time Elise and I will again be together. And we will, unless some fragment of reason fails me. Or luck turns away.

There is always that, some false turn not of our own making. When my eyes open, Hebestreit is looking my way. He shifts quickly on his stool, back to his job.

'What is it now, *Oberfunkmaat*?'

'Nothing, sir.'

I stare at him bent closer to his devices. I leave it at that. We have learned to allow each other our private moments. It is the sign of an able crew, is it not? Our lovers would want to know we allow each other that.

Mrs. Shiers is singing now, a lullaby for her boy. Hers is not the most soothing of voices, but it is gentle in its own way, and it is a mother's, settling over the others in the lifeboat as if they are children in need of reassurance.

Your mother shakes the branches small
Lovely dreams in showers fall
Sleep, baby, sleep

Charlotte's hand lies outside the blanket covering her. Hank strokes her hand gently to warm it and then presses it against his cheek. He brushes aside the strands of hair that lie in tangles across her face. Charlotte is a sorrowful sight, but she's made it this far, and Hank believes he can help her make it to daylight, to the time rescuers will surely arrive.

At that moment John stirs. He is about to say something but winces at a sudden pain in his leg. He leans forward, sputters a curse. Then settles back again. His eyes stay open, fixed on Charlotte. He wants to be holding her hand.

And again Mrs. Shiers starts to sob.

Alex pays her no mind. It's a good while yet to daylight, and those in the best shape have got to help the others keep out the cold. John insists he can stand a lot more, shuddering with every word.

Hank moves closer to Charlotte.

They are a damned tormented lot, clumped together by darkness and uncertainty. There's silence, and for the moment it deepens. It lingers.

A brittle humming arises, of no decipherable tune. From Charlotte. No one stirs, the lull an encouragement for it to gain strength.

John lifts his head, then sinks back again.

Hank starts to hum quietly in unison. Mrs. Shiers nods her approval, her eyes fixed on Charlotte.

The nurse stirs some more. It is doing her good.

Mrs. Shiers reaches out to her, enclosing Charlotte's hands with her own.

Think of all the people she and her friend had nursed, how hard they worked to make them well.

Mrs. Shiers sings, her voice no better than before.

Our God, our help in ages past. Our hope for years to come.
Our shelter from the stormy blast…

This one Alex knows. Lundrigan makes a third. Then Charlotte, a wisp of a voice, hardly audible.

It is the most peace they've found aboard the boat.

Alex turns to John to prod him to join in.

His head is sunk to one side, his eyes shut. He's no longer shivering.

Jesus.

Alex clutches the fellow's head in his hands. There's nothing but a weak moan.

Hank starts rubbing his arms. The others spur him on.

The commotion disrupts Charlotte from her stupor. She holds out her blanket. Hank wraps it around him.

She tells Hank to get as close as he can to his face, to cup his hands and breathe out so John will breathe in his warm air.

She knows what she's doing. She's a nurse.

Hank bends his head forward.

'Closer. Closer.'

'Damn it all.'

John coughs, faintly.

'Keep it up. Don't stop now.'

The coughing turns stronger. The fellow opens his eyes to discover Hank's face in his. He grimaces.

'Hang on. Hang on.'

Eventually the worst is past. It is over and done with.

They sink back into themselves, relieved, few words between them.

Lundrigan prayed through it all and now his faith is stronger than ever. They're alive for a purpose. They must be.

For Alex it's fear the worst and thank God for the rest. Never once has he thought he might not see his wife and family again.

Sobs again penetrate the calm. It stirs Charlotte to utter a few words, slow and fitful, unheard. She's praying for Leonard.

'It's all in God's hands.' There's a finality to Lundrigan that no one welcomes.

Hank has been praying, too.

It is almost 7 a.m. The sea has begun to uncover itself. And with it the ever-louder question of what the *Grandmère* will do.

What will Cuthbert do? It is a judgment that tears at him as none before.

For the hour since the last depth charges he has searched in vain. Is the U-boat on the ocean floor, mortally wounded, seawater slowly replacing oxygen, crewman after crewman struggling to his end?

Cuthbert is not so innocent. The U-boat more likely sits in wait, somewhere deep, motors idling, outsmarting the ASDIC. If Cuthbert turns to the survivors, will it surface and set its sights on what he will be making of his ship—a sitting duck? It wrenches him one way, then the other. There is no procedure for this one. No orders on the order book.

Or has the U-boat slipped away to the open ocean? To where it can revel freely in its conquest. Cuthbert has no way of knowing and nothing to guide him but instinct.

Instinct can be a grim collaborator. The Canadian Navy puts no stock in it.

What the murk reveals is the aimless wash of debris. Scraps of wood, a sole lifebelt, an empty life raft. All drifting toward the *Grandmère*.

It is the final prod. There is no denying Cuthbert an answer any longer.

'Reverse engines. Change coordinates. Prepare the scramble net.' Pray they are still alive.

I HAVE FAITH IN THE CANADIAN. HE WILL NOT DENY HIS survivors.

Here, at this depth, it is fiercely quiet. The ferry has creaked her last. One day perhaps she will share the ocean floor with the vessel that put her there. The chances are in its favour. It would be foolish to deny it. And one thing I am not, Father, is a fool. Fools dream of war, but when I allowed myself to dream, it was of animals swept in wild colours, unbelievably real. And time and again of a woman, and of a son, of the hopes I would have for him. Just like you must have dreamt, Father, of the hopes you had for your son, during your days of war. We both have had our dreams.

Her eyes are closed. It draws her closer to her boy. Her prayers are private now, strands of stiffened hope in the daybreak.

Others peer into it, past the mists, to a quieter sea than they had imagined. A lifeboat? Rafts? The most earnest stares turn skyward.

Her husband expects her. He knows no different. The hopes for Leonard drift as inconstantly as the few birds that skim the surface of the sea. When she does open her eyes, she allows these creatures to possess her, in the way they disappear and reappear, measuring a way into dawn.

By sunrise the chill has set into everyone aboard, but weighed against the promise of rescue, they are stronger. Alex keeps the boat as steady as he is able in waters that have turned choppy.

Abruptly his words shoot overhead.

In time they all catch the distant sight of the airplane, its sound barely perceptible, their ears straining madly for it.

They wave anything they can. They turn the blankets to taut, oversized flags.

It is sizable now and growing steadily closer, on course to fly directly overhead. They wield the blankets frantically. The airplane's two propellers roar, atop broad wings splayed across a patch of sky.

A blue circle enclosing a red maple leaf. At last, the Canadians. The airplane drops flame floats so the *Grandmère* will fix on their position.

Hank whoops into the sky.

Alex barks at him to stay calm like they all must do until there's something certain.

Hank sits and rubs his hands together. Just burning daylight.

For the first time, they can make out others who have survived. There's a raft, unmistakable in the distance off their stern. Alex is certain there are people aboard. Too far away to call, but when he strains again to hear, he is sure it is survivors, singing together.

Nearer my God to Thee. He is sure it is.

Lundrigan is desperate for them to add their voices. *Nearer to Thee*.

And not long after, the bow of the *Grandmère* breaks through the mist. She comes to loom among the living and the dead.

A ship's searchlight sweeps to their lifeboat and the six aboard.

They're alive. Every one of them.

FEBRUARY 1943

No Atlantic crossing had been easier, no approach to the coast of France less infested with Tommies. Nonetheless, it was sweet relief to slip past Port-Louis, sweep up the Le Blavet to Lorient and into one of the bunkers. Three meters of steel-reinforced concrete, a haven bombs could never defile.

For sixteen hours U-69 had perched inert above the sunken ferry. Except for one furtive scan at periscope depth, we resigned ourselves to outlast the day, not knowing when the surface would be cleared of its survivors, and if more inept Canadians would show up and strike it lucky with their depth charges. We dared not claim victory until we were far from it all.

We escaped under the renewed cover of darkness, and surfaced to find the seas incredibly vacant. The escort was long gone, with no more sign of the Canadian Navy, except for a faint signal from our Metox. When it did finally grow louder, we changed course, looking vigilantly though the binoculars to a distant moonlit coil of water that the night before had blazed in chaos. Hardly ever do we have the dubious luxury of second thought. Routinely, there's only the blast and the mad panic to get away.

Hagemann showed what passed for a smile. His equivalent of a roaring grin. He was well satisfied, and so was I, though the intoxication of battle was past.

Its consequences remained. A commander worth his rank takes no satisfaction in human torment. Satisfaction at the enemy vessel at the bottom of the seas, yes. It is war after all.

We were two months at sea. The men were feverish to see an end to it. I could not fault them for that. The ever-growing stench tends to infest one's zeal.

Odd that the coast of Newfoundland compelled me still. Spare moments behind the curtain to my quarters had seen me sketching it from memory. And on the bridge, as if it were possible to ignore the dissonance, I imagined past the broad expanse of rock that sculpted the waterline, stared inland and for the moment lost myself ashore.

'Enjoying the view?' Hagemann inquired. It deadened the spell.

It was with that view we loaded our last torpedo, then set off to find a use for it. On October 20, it struck the ore carrier *Rose Castle*, only to fall away unexploded. A fucking dud, as Hagemann termed it, several times. Even so, no one despaired. For good reason, as time and U-518 would tell.

U-518—commanded by my good friend Friedrich-Wilhelm Wissmänn, mate from Crew 35. Fredy *Wissmännchen* we called him. He was a smart bugger despite his size. I remembered that we are almost the exact same age, born but one day apart. At Dänholm I would get a birthday pummeling from the other cadets, and get my own back the following day.

Incredibly, it was December 15th, in the midst of a drunken birthday stupor in Lorient, when who should show up but

Wissmänn, back that very day from his first patrol as commander.

His smile outshone his scruffiness. The bearded young reprobate had struck six ships, sunk four: 30,000 GRT. I had two patrols behind me and had reached only half that.

'Beginner's bloody luck, Wissmänn.' Smiling as friends must do.

'The last was a Yankee tanker,' he declared, by that time almost as drunk as I was, 'filled to the hatches and heading for Iceland. The bastard never got past Newfoundland.'

U-518 salvaged the captain and chief officer, took them aboard as prisoners, while the rest of the crew scattered in lifeboats. 'And good fucking luck to them.'

Wissmänn was on top of the world, and I was halfway there. I told him of my own prize, the Cabot Strait ferry. And eventually it came to light that the *Rose Castle*, which had taken our dud of a torpedo, was the same ship U-518 had shot to hell while it was anchored off Newfoundland, loaded with iron ore and waiting to join a convoy.

'By God, Wissmänn, you're a slick goddamn shot.' The beer and schnapps doing what they were meant to do.

We made a rousing night of it, Wissmänn and I and Werner Witte, another slacker from Crew 35. He had managed 24,000 GRT off the coast of Morocco.

Over the months since the *Kriegsmarine* had taken over the port of Lorient, a building on its outskirts had been fashioned into a refuge for its officers, for those who had done with Madame and her girls. It was a chaotic showplace, with its plush sofas, red velvet curtains, and ineptly stenciled grape vines circling a stage where, from time to time, moribund musicians tackled swing. A trio of buxom French women had been commandeered to deliver drinks and generally relieve the boredom of men whose time ashore was only ever temporary. Witte's next patrol was scheduled for the following week. In all likelihood he'd be spending his Christmas chasing some convoy, wondering what gift the Tommies had in mind for him and his crew. Already this year more than eighty U-boats have cashed it in, half of them since October. The benefits of a flatulent beer hall are not to be underestimated.

'What's for you then, Gräf? You have a few weeks left.'

'Dresden for Christmas. Paris.'

'Ah, Paris. Get yourself fucked in Paris,' said Wissmänn. 'You'll want the recollection, no matter your next patrol.'

'You always were a practical man, Fredy.'

'Gräf has had his fair share already, or so the rumours go. Here in Lorient. And homegrown.'

I could do better than blush. 'Hell, Witte, you reek of jealousy.'

He let loose a loud disclaimer, adding, 'Beware the pitfalls of a love affair, Gräf. There is no room in the *Kriegsmarine* for heartache.'

I let them have their fun. To deny it would only fuel their ridicule.

Luckily the musicians had returned to the stage and provided a new focus for the drunken insults. I was only too happy to join in.

The French girls saw it as their duty to protect the musicians, and at the same time outflank any potential damage to the club. Beer glasses had been known to fly, light fixtures left dangling by their wires. I generally escaped the bar when I sensed the situation getting out of hand, but in this case there would be no getting past Wissmänn and Witte.

Then Hagemann made a sudden appearance, adding new colour to the scene, the second watch officer in tow. For the moment I thought a friendship had taken hold. But I soon saw that Umbeck was so drunk he could not stand upright without Hagemann's grip on his upper arm. The unlikely pair planted themselves at a table near the bar.

When he caught sight of me, Hagemann stiffened involuntarily, fighting against looking anything but the incorruptible Exec. He was plainly unable to keep up the pretense, his glass falling short of the span from the table to his mouth. Beer splattered down the front of his uniform.

I couldn't resist a broad grin and a raised arm, a limp gesture that only confused him further. I realized he had taken it for a slight to his Nazi creed, something which was bound to serve neither of us very well. I hoped his drunkenness might dull his memory, but it was only hope.

We kept our distance. As for Umbeck, he had, by this time, fallen forward, his face immobile on the table. I grinned a second time, but turned in the direction of my fellow captains, who were too drunk to concern themselves with anything except getting drunker.

Soon, Witte was singing *Das ist die Berliner Luft*, rising to such enthusiasm that he took to his feet, fists clenched, arms swinging rigidly to the tune. The chorus scaled to its climax—*'Luft! Luft! Luft!'*—before invigorating the next verse and prompting the good captain to push aside his chair and begin a march around the table. One by one the stage musicians fell victim to his volume and slouched back in their chairs.

'Ja-ja! Ja-ja! Ja, ja, ja, ja! Das ist die Berliner Luft, Luft, Luft!'

Three times around the table and he had gathered a crew eager to prance along behind him, arms swinging and feet high-stepping in unison. Witte, the Berliner, leading the vocal charge, his reinforcements rounded out each chorus with a resounding *'Luft, Luft, Luft!'*

It was an alcohol-fired, noble sight, bound to raise the spirits of the most fatalistic commanders, among whose numbers I might have placed myself were it not for Elise.

Our love-making saved me. There had been times when the thought that I would soon captain a third U-boat patrol came close to overpowering my self-control. Not that I wouldn't have gone—that was without question—but a slip in eagerness to take it on would have been inexcusable to the crew. The men depend on unequivocal focus for the kill, absolute belief in survival. Otherwise who would dare go aboard, who would dare have the hatch close after them and follow a man about to sink fifty of their kind into the brine?

Elise sensed my apprehension. I was not the person she had sat across from at the terrace of *Le Grand Café* on the evening I had last seen her, nor the person whose hands she had laughingly squirmed from after our final, impassioned kiss. She had walked away reluctantly, then looked back, then came running back knowing she could never satisfy me at that moment, but as much as promising me she would when next we found each other.

'Ulrich,' she said, 'what is it?'

It was the matter of time. A captain doesn't step away from the calamitous life aboard a U-boat as readily as he might have done after his first patrol.

'Was it something that happened?'

Something to be pinpointed, a visceral moment that played and replayed against me? What matter, for there was nothing she could hope to understand, or that anyone but a U-boatman could understand. Nothing that bore explaining. Not to Elise. Not Elise.

She was there to turn me aside from all that. To encourage me to fall in love. As if the war could go on without us, as if inevitably we would go on without it.

Perhaps I was not giving her the credit she was due. A nurse after all, she had dressed the ravages of bullets and bombs. Looked into the faces of the dead. Sent letters to their mothers.

I smiled across the table at the restaurant of *L'Hôtel du Lapin Blanc,* but said nothing. The hotel was not far from the sand of Larmor-Plage. We had progressed to hours walking the beach, for the most part deserted. The time for vacationers was long past. What drew us back to the shoreline—bundled we were against the chill of mid-November—could only be its tameness, its beauty, the muted breath as the seawater coated the shore. We indulged the fantasies of summer.

The hotel and restaurant, too, had but a few guests, another table of Germans only. The waiter was exceptionally courteous, though, of course, there was no telling what was said in the confines of the kitchen. He appeared to appreciate the business. The mussels were excellent.

The others were the left-over administration at Kernével. Dönitz had transferred U-boat headquarters from Lorient to Paris in the spring, but a contingent of officers remained, to oversee the port's operations. One or two persisted in glancing our way. I recognized the fellow who had led me to Madame after my first patrol. His jealousy was thinly disguised. It gave me untold pleasure.

Elise kept a distance, wary of revealing any affection toward me. The Nazi gentlemen now feigned disinterest, but who could say what files were kept on the nurses under their jurisdiction. My hand stretched to the middle of the table was slowly withdrawn.

Her glance into my eyes caught a sly wink, forcing her lips together to keep from smiling.

'You're ravishing, sweetheart,' I whispered. 'Let me plant a horde of kisses on those lips.' For the benefit of the other table, I could have been discussing the weather. Elise looked away, her unreadable mask turning crimson.

'A droll scamp pays a price,' she murmured soberly.

'Truly?'

'In time.'

'I'll take my chances. Have I ever mentioned that you have the most appetizing neck?'

'Eat your mussels.'

I smiled and returned to the bowl in front of me. The mussels went very well with the *muscadet*. Elise had chosen scallops instead. Prelude to the main course—monkfish in a tomato and white-wine sauce, brought straight to the table in its cooking skillet.

She was warming to the moment, despite the distraction. We wisely continued to drink wine while lingering through dessert.

'The Bretons call it *Kouigne-Amann*,' said Elise.

'Sounds threatening.'

'Butter cake.'

Overture to something sweeter. She was reading my mind.

I nodded to the officers on our way out. We had planned to outlast them, but they became increasingly loud and, rather than have to listen to whatever boorish remarks might spew from them should they get any drunker, I convinced Elise it was better we made our escape.

It was a miscalculation.

'Well, then good night, *Oberleutnant zur See*.' He was older and outranked me, but spent his days filling a desk and pushing paper to Berlin.

'Good night.' I saluted, anxious to have done with them.

Elise and I were well past the table when he sang out, 'You are in a rush, *Oberleutnant*. For good reason, I assume.' Their laughter clogged the room.

A more outright bastard than I suspected. Now that Dönitz had gone there was no one to keep their bloated heads in line. No one to make it perfectly clear that if the *Kriegsmarine* were to bring glory to the Reich, then the officers who actually seal themselves in the U-boats would be the ones to fucking do it. Not the idiot backslappers smoking cigars in the lounges of Kernével.

Elise held my arm. 'Don't, Ulrich. It'll do no good.'

I strained to free myself.

'No. It will make it worse for me.'

She was right. We passed out of the room without another word. The laughter had not subsided. Damn, drunken asses.

We took to the veranda overlooking the shoreline, Elise's arm tightly against me. The air was stiff with cold, an abrupt infusion.

In the dark, the sea was foreboding, oddly more so onshore. It was not the time to think of returning. There was more to fill the night.

A U-boatman aims to fill his nights with memories. As much for the reminders as the delirium of the moment. For something to carry him for weeks and months through the narrow fragment of space that is his circumstance.

Elise knew as much. There were hardly the preliminaries, only as little as I needed. And when I came it was as if suffering had ceased, as if the whole of me had gathered for that single moment. I wanted it to crystallize, to be captured forever, knowing I could have it again and again.

She held to me in the end, her legs tightly around mine, locking against me as much of herself as it was imaginable to give. I ardently surrendered.

It was more romantic the second time.

And when we lay together naked, her body curved into mine, an arm wrapped into my chest, that was the beauty in it. Too soon the dawn was unfolding outside, the inevitable next day making itself known.

I stared far-off. Elise woven through the distance, painfully indefinite.

I knew I need not be so true. A U-boatman gathers his story and I can let it sing as loudly as the next man.

The days and nights in Lorient were all for Elise. If we were not together, I was wishing we were. She had her duties, and they were interminable at times, but then she would steal a few hours and we would devote ourselves to each other as if there had never been a divide. I worked at finding a way back to the person she had first known, a sincere approximation at least.

We had *Le Grande Café*, and soon a secluded section of it. Elise decided against relating the dramas at the hospital, and we chatted sparingly about the lives we had before the war. What we had most of all was each other, the food and wine, the scraps of laughter, the momentary brush of commitment. We hardly dared let it blossom.

The waiter, hesitant at first to be anything but silently efficient, began making comments about what he perceived as a charmed romance.

'*Monsieur*,' he said as we took our seats, '*vous avez bien choisi*.'

Elise translated when he had moved off, adding, 'he means the café.'

I thought not, and smiled broadly at him when he returned. It did encourage me to order a more expensive bottle of wine. We came to have a particular fondness for their seafood *crêpes*, and after enough visits the waiter no longer bothered with a menu, and instead noted enthusiastically what had been caught that day and would make an especially good filling for *crêpes*.

I was under no illusion. The French hated us Germans for having invaded their country. But I did think the fellow had found something in the pair of us to enjoy. We weren't demons. I wasn't out to please him, but who likes to share a meal under a black cloud. He went so far as to tell us his name when we asked—Claude, though he couldn't bring himself to use ours when we offered them.

Elise had a fondness for the language, and what of it she knew she seemed to speak without an accent, to my untrained ear at least. Claude appreciated this, no doubt tired of the invaders murdering his native tongue. Elise found herself in his good graces even more when she asked him for the pronunciation of words she didn't know from the chalkboards.

'*Chenin, Mademoiselle. Chenin blanc. Un cépage typique de la région de la Loire.*'

It was more than she had wished for, but his enthusiasm was not lost on her.

We returned regularly to the café, each time more relaxed than the one before. Claude made no pretense of his liking for Elise, and I was the added beneficiary of his attention. He pulled wines from the cellar that never seemed to be on the chalkboards, meals arrived with complimentary side dishes. Each time on our leaving he bid us a *bonne soirée*.

It was tough to unravel. The French were not to be trusted. It was long suspected that the Frenchmen hired as dock workers to repair damaged U-boats were guilty of sabotage, to judge by the parade of boats back into Lorient with faulty valves, oil leaks, and electrical malfunctions. In fact the Frenchmen had been replaced by *Volksdeutsche*, ethnic Germans brought in from Eastern Europe. The problems lessened, but didn't vanish, leaving Headquarters forever uncertain just who to trust.

The day came when Elise left for a visit to her family home in Munich. My own mother and father in Dresden had been anxious to see me and there was no longer good reason to put off the journey. With Elise away, I generated some enthusiasm for the reunion. It was the holidays, and Christmas would be a diversion.

Since first entering Dänholm, an increasing distance had grown between my parents and I. The *Kriegsmarine* had shaped me into someone they didn't always recognize, and now, as U-boat captain, their fear for my safety had compounded the situation. The war had aged them, and I sensed they had begun to look on me as the son they might never see again.

The Reich ran special trains for its military from France into Germany, and spared no comforts, at least in food and beer. For some aboard—limbs missing, minds deeply scarred, bodies imprisoned on stretchers—the homecoming would be permanent. Their immediate despair was lost to the sweat and swagger of the others aboard.

The rail cars reserved for officers were less riotous. Our talk sobered us. The Americans had entered the war, and for the first while their ships ran into what some of us liked to call the American Shooting Season. Not quite up to the GRT of the Happy Time of 1940, but rather good jazz nonetheless. Unfortunately, the

Americans had smartened up and in recent months their tonnage sent to the cellar had slackened. Submarine warfare has its ups and downs as we like to say.

I leaned against the window frame and looked out on the passing countryside. It was bleaker than when I had last seen it. Crueler. There had been heavy rains and the farmyards were grey and squalid in the mud. In need of a firmer hand. Occasionally an old man or a woman with a child clinging at her skirts stood in a doorway and stared emotionless as the train passed. On one farm a sullen boy, about sixteen I guessed, raised a hand to us. When a soldier in the car ahead tossed an unopened bottle of beer from the train and into the bushes, the boy scurried towards it, and my last view of him was with his arm over his head, the unbroken bottle waving in the air.

Farming had to be a grievous existence with their men in North Africa and now Russia. From what we gathered, the battle for Stalingrad had not gone well, with heavy losses on both sides. Hundreds of thousands some were saying. I had cousins on the Russian Front. I counted myself the better off.

During the last few hours past Nuremberg I slept. When we pulled into Dresden Hauptbahnhof it was late in the afternoon. I had sent word ahead that I was coming, but there was no way of knowing if the message had been received. The station was generally deserted, except for the few lethargic troops with time on their hands. Most trains must have been using Neustadt station instead.

I dropped my bag partway along the platform and lit a cigarette. There was no notion of arriving home, even though I had been in the station countless times. I drew deeply on the cigarette and looked to the far end of a platform where I could see a train being boarded. It was an odd scene, with none of the usual exchanges between passengers and relatives coming to see them off. Soldiers stood guard. They surrounded weary, shrunken passengers and shuffled them aboard. I stood and watched, uncertain what I was witnessing.

I rid myself of the cigarette and took up the bag. There was still no sign of my father. I wasn't surprised. Then, just as I passed into the grand concourse, with the immense, high curve of its ceiling, I saw him in the distance, the sole person walking the wasteland of polished stone floor toward me. He stepped awkwardly, seemingly in an attempt to remain as noiseless as possible.

I put down the bag and waited for him, holding out my hand as he approached. He seized it and with his other hand took up the bag.

'We must go now.' He had yet to smile. I had not seen him for almost a year.

He led me back the way he had come, as quickly as he could without making it appear we were rushing. We approached the guard at the main entrance.

'My son,' he told him. 'On leave from the *Kriegsmarine*.' The fellow nodded and to me he raised his right arm rigidly. I nodded and walked on.

I asked my father about the train I had seen. He shook his head.

'Who are they?'

He had no answer still.

I expected a walk to his Maybach. The car had been a great source of pride, even though by then it must have been a decade old. The walk was to a tram instead. Even a taxi was out of the question. He told me that a taxi had to be approved by the police. We spent a half hour waiting on the platform before the tram arrived and much longer still before reaching our neighbourhood.

Father said little. Occasionally someone recognized him but they barely acknowledged each other. I sat in silence, my bag crowded in my lap. I wanted to ask about the car but sensed it was an embarrassment. Eventually he volunteered, 'There is no gas to be had.'

I could see cars on the roads. Not many, but enough that his words seemed an excuse.

'I gave it up,' he said. 'They needed vehicles. They liked the model.'

The Gestapo I assumed. The war had turned Dresden into a city of secrets.

Father being a doctor, we had lived more comfortably than most. Now everyone was expected to make sacrifices in the effort to win the war. It was not enough that he had given his son.

Just how much the welfare of my parents had suffered didn't strike me until we reached the apartment. Mother, only ever a slight woman, appeared at the door looking particularly thin. When I embraced her I could feel just how thin. She had tried her best—the emerald green dress with the lace collar that always suited her, her hair braided, then coiled and pinned at the back of her head. She smiled, holding back tears as she led me inside.

I came to see that Mother spent most of her day in the sitting room and the kitchen, while Father was away at his clinic. The radiators in several rooms of the apartment had been closed off to conserve heat, the door to their bedroom opened only a half hour before bedtime to allow some of the rationed heat to escape into it. The door to the lavatory was open a fraction, enough to keep the water pipes from freezing.

'Your father insists we cut back, even with our son in the house. Coal is not restricted. I don't understand.'

'It is only a matter of time, Annemarie. Bolshevik prisoners doing the jobs of proper miners. Should anyone be surprised production is down? We must do our part. They notice these things.'

Mother would take the matter no further. She had raised it in my presence, thinking he might relent, even for a short while. She wasn't about to give up trying, despite the fact there was only the barest hope that Father would change his mind. I was five minutes in the apartment and already I was set between them.

My old room was there for me to use, but I calculated it had been so long without heat that it would take days to dislodge the cold from the mattress and bedclothes. My parents were using the room to store a meager supply of vegetables and other perishables, the combination of which left an odd odour. I stood for a moment gazing at the pair of paintings of the Bavarian countryside that had been hanging in the same places on the wall since I was a schoolboy.

I suggested I sleep on the sofa. They would oblige me.

I was not hungry, but she had prepared *Kartoffelpuffer*. There were generally potatoes, she told me, but nothing to make the applesauce. I did better, surprising them with the contents of my suitcase, together with the *Führer-Paket* given to each man at our first train stop after we crossed the border into Germany. The Führer's Christmas package to each military man aboard.

They had not seen good sausage in months. Such choice sardines much longer. Chocolate and honey and almonds. They stared at it on the table as if it were a danger to consume, as if there would be a price to pay for displaying such luxury.

'Eat,' I insisted.

'We must save some for Frieda.' She was my mother's closest friend, a widow who lived not far along the street. 'She is not well, Ulrich.'

'Of course.'

'Old age setting in,' said my father, decisively. He and Frieda had had their differences.

Mother shook her head, again close to tears. 'She lost her Emil.'

Her grandson and I had been in the same class to graduate *Gymnasium*.

'He fell in Russia.'

We had taken separate paths, I into the navy, he eventually the infantry. In later years we no longer encountered each other, yet mother always wrote of him as if Emil and I had remained friends.

'I am not surprised.' It was the truth. So many of the foot soldiers had died in Russia.

Father latched onto my measured response. 'An *Oberleutnant* for certain had he lived.'

'The Führer could have done better than to invade Russia,' I said.

I could feel the chill in my father's eyes. No patriot questioned the Führer, even in the confines of his own home. Surely not a man of the *Kriegsmarine*.

'And the Jews,' said my mother. She had seen an opening and snatched it. 'We have heard the worse.'

'You have heard nothing, Annamarie. Rumours, that is all. Jews have been relocated.'

'There are no Jews left in the city, Ulrich, unless they are married to someone who is not a Jew. Even they must walk the streets with a yellow star pinned to their chests. For why, I ask you. Your friend Josef, his mother wears a star. She dares not say a word to me for fear she will be, as your father puts it, *relocated*. Like her son. They sent Josef away. His star did him no good. Why, do you think?'

'One day you will have us in trouble with your questions,' Father declared, no longer suppressing his anger. 'Then it will be too late.'

That night, with my parents in their bedroom, I sat on the sofa, blankets stalling the draft, smoking a cigarette. The apartment windows were tightly curtained with black fabric, but I chose to sit in the dark.

The train I had seen at the station was as I suspected. Mother guessed it was on its way to Theresienstadt. No one comes back, she said.

Josef was also a friend, before I went to Dänholm. Not when I came back on holiday. He had his other friends then, and I had a different way of going about the world. I would see him and we would shake hands at first, but then he had his own life. I had the navy, and Jews had no part in the navy.

I was reminded of Teddy Suhren. Teddy always had a joke, about Jews some of them. We'd laugh, even though we all had Jewish friends before Dänholm. And for a few of us they were our best friends. After a while we didn't admit to that, and by the time we had finished our training, we each had other best friends. And Teddy still had his jokes. His repertoire had expanded. The last time I saw him he said, 'So Hitler and Göring were standing on top of the Berlin Radio Tower, and Hitler says, I want to do something to put a smile on German faces. Göring looks at him and says, How about you jump?'

Teddy could get away with it. Teddy and his 95,000 GRT.

I tell my mother the joke, when there is just the two of us. She doesn't laugh. She says, 'How about they both jump?' and goes back to sorting her ration tickets.

I have yet to understand my father. He had known many Jews. Perhaps not to count among his friends, but he was often in their company, in the hospitals, in the streets. I often heard him speak of Josef's father before he died. We went to his funeral, the three of us.

He has put that out of his mind. He avoids all talk about Jews and I see no use in pressing him. He has himself, his wife, and his son to worry about. It would seem that is enough. He has left the Jews to their own fate.

The next day I am walking to see my former instructor, Wilhelm Lachnit, and I can see that Dresden has done the same. I passed a bent old man battling to hold his ragged coat closed, his posture half-hiding a yellow star. He should have been taking the tram, but it is forbidden. Following behind him, taunting him, were three boys in uniform, black neck scarves, belts across their chests, swastika armbands. Three pristine Hitler Youths.

'Stand tall, old man. Are you ashamed of what you are?'

Others passed by, not willing to involve themselves, pretending they noticed nothing.

'Pig man, you are a disgrace,' declared the boldest. 'Fall down and smash your head and be done with it.' The other two howled.

'Leave him alone.'

They were about to say something when I produced my *Soldbuch*, flipped it open to the photograph ID, and stuck it in their faces. 'Heil!' Their arms whipped in salute.

I sent the clowns on their way with a wave of my hand. The old man hobbled on, as if nothing had happened, as if he were unaware of anything but the sidewalk in front of him.

I had not seen Herr Lachnit for several years. He had moved from the apartment studio I would go to for art instruction, and I was not sure I would ever discover his whereabouts. My inquiries at the Dresden Academy were met with cold indifference, and only as I left the building in frustration did someone call to me from behind and offer his help.

'Herr Lachnit left the Academy on bad terms. He deserved better.' The fellow quickly gave me an address and turned away. I had no idea who he was, and it had been obvious he didn't want me to know.

My former instructor, the man who led me into what he called "the conundrum of art," barely recognized me. I was not the teen-aged boy who had shown promise during the art classes at school, who had taken the tram once a week to his studio for special instruction arranged by my mother, where he demonstrated tech-niques of line drawing, where he showed me his ways with colour. He himself looked considerably older. What was he? Just past forty perhaps.

The tuft of black, wavy hair that he always kept immaculately combed had gone limp. He wore a shirt that had once been white and a tie coarsely knotted, under a heavy coat to keep out the cold. It was in desperate need of cleaning. It had once hung on a much more robust frame. 'Ulrich,' he said finally.

'I have brought you a few things.' A few things from France that I had kept aside— salami, jam, biscuits. He brightened at the sight of them.

'Sit down. It has been a long time.'

I removed my gloves and loosened my coat. We sat and smoked Gitanes. Surrounding us was years of his work, in various stages of composition—a thick clutter of sketches, gouaches, oils. The paintings, mostly portraits and still lifes, filled an otherwise doom-ful studio with strong, defiant colour. It was because of Herr Lachnit that I had come to know the work of Franz Marc. The two painters chose different subjects, but Lachnit had followed some of the path set by Marc. He had also followed his good friends Dix and Felixmüller, and half-hidden among the easels and drawing tables was a small press where he made woodcuts and etchings.

But it was in line drawing that he found his greatest pleasure. That had been the starting point when I first came to him and it would remain our focus right to the end, until I finally left home for my training. 'Harmony,' he had said to me in the beginning. 'In the midst of disorder you must be sensitive to that core of harmony.' There was a quiet melancholic peace in his portraits, but even at that, some were at odds with the Nazi judgment of art.

Four of his drawings had been confiscated from galleries, and, together with the work of the other artists he most admired, mocked in exhibitions throughout the country. He had been singled out and imprisoned, and when he was released he fell under the constant eye of the Gestapo.

Stripped of his livelihood, he was determined to make art, even if it forced him into poverty and into odd jobs to keep body and soul together. I felt pity for him, but pity was not something he would tolerate.

In fact if there was pity being openly displayed it was for me. 'Ulrich, this war is madness.' It had come so plainly that I knew among his fellows it had to be common talk.

He caught himself. Trust was not so easily demonstrated anymore. He stopped, feeling for my reaction.

'I didn't join up expecting it. War is what it is. My job as it turned out.' I was holding back. Captains were only ever lauded for manning U-boats. He knew that much.

'Courage,' he said. 'It takes that. Fearlessness.'

He meant it, I assumed. Not that it mattered. The man was exhausted by what had been done to him, and I had no reason to expect anything more. Why had I come at all? Why had I not wished him well and left again?

Germany is rife with contradiction, with men willing to dismiss the sacrifice of others, the sacrifice of their very lives many of them. By what logic? The logic of brush to canvas?

Cannot the two coexist? I was stirred by the single-mindedness I saw around me. I know well Herr Lachnit's passion. But I have come to know the fierce passion of men for survival on the open seas, the passion to fight or be laid waste.

'An artist is an instrument of faith,' he said, as if I were still a youth of sixteen sketching next to him. I had not forgotten those words. He had used them again and again.

Faith. I know the crux of faith. I know faith in the men standing with me, as much in peril as I am. I know that more than the refuge of home.

As meager as home might be. Herr Lachnit offered me coffee and brought it in a chipped cup stained by repeated use. It was sham, *ersatz* coffee, made from God knows what. I sipped it to be generous, and considered whether he brought it to make a point of just how burdened he was.

'The *Kriegsmarine* treats its men well?'

'Very well.'

'You deserve it. As long as it lasts.'

The bitter edge did not augur well for more than a perfunctory chat about very little. Herr Lachnit, I had thought, would have been thankful for a diversion from his grim routine.

If a man cannot open himself to the broader world I am left to question the wisdom of condemning it outright. A harsh judgment, but then I have been forced to endure my own share of harsh judgments.

When I rose to leave, it was with regret at having come. 'Goodbye, then. I hope your circumstance improves.'

'What did you expect of your visit, Ulrich?'

I shook his hand. 'To relive your obsession, perhaps. To see what became of it.'

'Did it meet your expectations?'

'It appears I'm not to know.' I buttoned my coat and fitted my hands into my gloves. 'Art is a conundrum, Herr Lachnit.'

I walked away and made for the street.

I was anxious to be done with home. A man who lives by danger is at odds with people who are in constant dread of it. Dresden has weakened at its core. It is no more the city of my youth, but a paranoid facsimile, a city sunk in malaise without the will to fight its way out. It should have considered itself fortunate not to have suffered the bombing that Hamburg and Cologne had to endure.

As much as Mother wanted me to stay even a day longer, I was resolved that once Christmas Day passed I would take the train to Paris. Christmas Eve had turned to a battle of wills. Mother was refusing the police directive that Christmas trees must no longer bear a star such as the one that she had forever set in place on the top branch of our tree. Only the swastika was allowable.

Father had tried to make a case for not having a tree at all, not if it was going to cause so much upset. His furrowed brow was clear indication they'd had this argument before. I suspected Mother reignited it for my benefit, once again to see where my allegiance lay. 'Surely the police have more to do than patrol neighbourhoods to report on the state of Christmas trees!'

'The swastika is ancient, a symbol of religion,' Father offered weakly. It sparked in my mother a fresh lament for what their lives had become.

With time, peace prevailed, enough that the tree was finally erected, though half the height of what I knew as a boy, and barren except for the candles in their tin holders and a few of the painted glass ornaments that had once brought Mother so much pleasure. She drew the last one from its box, adding bluntly, 'I suppose they have no problems with pinecones.'

All this for the sake of a Christmas tree. It was beyond me to deal with it.

Mother might have been denied her tree, but not her *Christstollen*. Baked as she had done every Christmas, even if she had to make do with the meager choice of dried fruit and nuts. In fact, on the outside the bread looked even finer than in other years, revenge for the dearth of ingredients inside. Shaped and covered in the powdered sugar she had been hoarding for months, it was made to resemble more than ever the swaddling clothes of the Christ Child.

Father bit into it as if he feared it might turn to bile in his mouth. Nothing was said even after I commented, 'Wonderful, Mother. Your reputation is intact.' A failed attempt at sounding like the boy who once had great fun teasing her.

Dresden *stollen* is acclaimed across Germany as the finest. The making of it was something my mother would approach with a seriousness that as a youth I thought bizarre, even if I gorged myself on the results. I tactlessly questioned why someone would put so much effort into the baking of a loaf of bread, when there were exceptional bakeries within short walking distance of our apartment. Except, Mother was Mother, and she had her priorities.

Now I could only admire her. It was a tradition she stubbornly held to at all costs. Dresden had a reputation to maintain. While the war tore at her and her city, the making of Christmas bread became a desperate assertion that there were still some things right with the world. *Christstollen* was one of them.

Christmas Day passed with little of its usual festivity. Uncle Wolfgang and Aunt Sophia came by, together with their son, Felix, a boy of thirteen who did nothing to remind me of myself when I was that age. He sat stiffly in a chair, in pants that he had outgrown, looking overly sober, as if there was nothing of any humour in life. He did take an acute interest in my career, listening intently to his father's flurry of questions, questions which I brought to a premature halt.

'A matter of naval security, Uncle.'

'Of course, Ulrich,' he said. 'Still, you are taking your life in your hands every time you close that hatch. A man cannot do any more for the homeland. The Reich has Churchill running scared. It is only a matter of time before we prevail.'

His optimism I could have done without, though I was willing to let it pass. Not so my mother.

'You are conveniently forgetting Russia, Wolfgang.'

'I am conveniently forgetting nothing.' It was obvious he had no time for the views of his brother's wife, especially when it interrupted discussion between men. His own wife knew better than to have an opinion. Aunt Sophia readjusted herself on the sofa and sipped more of her coffee, as putrid as it was. Neither did Felix open his mouth, not that he dared consider doing it.

It was a useful time to retrieve the half-bottle of cognac I had planned on revealing later, to follow the meal.

'Glasses, Mother. A toast is in order.' A toast to what exactly, I had no idea as I sought out my suitcase and retrieved the bottle.

Mother's set of hand-blown and painted cordial glasses initiated what festivity there was and the Courvoisier proved the crowning touch. For a few moments at least the war was set aside.

'A toast,' I said. 'To victory.' We all drank.

The men smiled and admired its quality. Nothing nearly as good had passed their lips for some time.

'To the birth of the Christ Child,' said my mother.

It unsettled the rest of us. A deliberate provocation that served no purpose.

JOHN STRIPPED DOWN, STRETCHED HIMSELF ON THE BED for the doctor to have his look. It hurt like hell, but the smile didn't budge. He swore up and down that the doctor should have no worries. He was coming along, perfect.

It fell on deaf ears. The doctor picked up the chart, returned the smile, and marked him down for another night in the Sydney hospital.

The next morning, word reached the hospital that the *Burgeo* was sailing to Newfoundland that same day, the first ferry to cross the Strait since the night the *Caribou* went down. Any survivor well enough to go could take passage. That would be John. There was a way back to Newfoundland and he wasn't about to be left behind.

His shoulder had been bruised black and blue, but there were no bones broken. The cut to his leg was healing and he had enough strength that the crutches got him where he needed to go.

It was not her decision, the nurse told him. If it was, he wouldn't be going anywhere. She offered an indulgent smile. She couldn't be blind to the fact he'd been up and down the hallway every half-hour and not once did he lose his balance.

Still, he had scoffed at every meal she put in front of him. No way was he anything but one pain-in-the-ass of a patient.

When the doctor made his rounds, John was dressed in the charity clothes that had been stashed in the locker adjacent to his bed. They were meant for somebody taller and with a bigger gut. The shoes fit, but whose diseased feet were in them last was his question.

John shut up and awaited the verdict. Whatever it took to get him out the door and aboard a ride to the ferry terminal in North Sydney.

The doctor took his time, studied John, amused at his eagerness. The doctor had taken to being chummy.

John was not one to lie around.

'Nightmares?'

He denied it. The nurse had a different story.

In the end, the doctor signed off on him. John was on the crutches and out the door before he changed his mind. Never gave the nurse a chance to dispense her good-bye.

The waiting room at the ferry terminal in North Sydney was crowded with survivors from the *Caribou*. Except for the few still in hospital or those who had figured out some other way of getting to Newfoundland. Lundrigan had taken an airplane to Gander. Most of them had no choice. It was the ferry or nothing.

The crossing would be in daylight this time and the Canadian Navy had its eyes open wider. There'd be an escort circling them. Not the *Grandmère*.

No matter what, Alex had it figured the Germans were long gone. The swine knew better than try it a second time.

Others had their doubts. John hobbled from person to person, assuring them it was all going to be fine. As if he had every reason to take on that job. The reason he had was Miss Fitzpatrick. He was doing what she would have done. Except there were no children left. Apart from young Leonard, all the others were dead, a good many of their parents with them. Leonard had been saved by a gunner from the Royal Canadian Artillery. The fellow discovered the child floating, aided by air trapped beneath his nightshirt. He snatched him from the water and passed him aboard a life raft.

Mrs. Shiers and her boy were still at the hospital. She was having a hard time. Yet she had her son, and eventually she would reunite with her husband, and together they would make a life for the boy.

William Strickland was off by himself in a corner, a man pounded mad because he was the only one in his family left alive. There was nothing John said to him that made it any easier.

Hank was there, tight with the other G.I.s. He had fought like a dog to save himself, John gave him that much. He came over and shook John's hand and that was alright. He wasn't saying much, which was just as well. John could do with not hearing any more of his accent.

He searched about until he found Charlotte. She was still in shock, but the Canadian Navy boys were keeping an eye on her. One of their own. They'd all heard her story. The body of her friend had been picked up and was in Port aux Basques, waiting for Charlotte to show up to make positive identification. John left Charlotte alone, though he had plenty he wanted to say to her. It would wait.

Take it one day at a time.

One day at a time, and thank God you're alive and go from there and after a while you're back to yourself.

He wanted to think it was that easy. It wasn't. It was all a bugger, some days more, some days less.

His plan was to make for home. Spend a few weeks in St. Anthony, let the leg heal, then take off again for St. John's and join up. That was the plan. It would take time, that was all. Time to get the leg back to what it had been and make sure the circus of his head was screwed on right.

He shared a cabin with Alex on the way over. Alex had it figured that John needed some place he could stretch out and take a load off the leg. The crossing started off rough. Alex wasn't saying much and there was nothing much to be said in any case.

After a while, lying in the bunk, staring at the ceiling, it got as bad as at the hospital. At the first sign of the wind dying back, John was out of the bunk, straight-legged up the stairs and into the lounge. Ready for the rum like he'd had in his mind since he came aboard.

Hank was there, no surprise. He came over to where John was sitting with his poker leg out in front of him. Hank offered to buy him a drink. Why not. Hank's offering, why fucking not.

He told him too bad about Buzz. He'd never said that face-to-face before. Hank said the same about Miss Fitzpatrick.

Had he heard the numbers? Over a hundred was what John had heard, a hundred and thirty maybe.

Hank said they beat the odds.

As far as John figured it, nobody beat any fucking odds. They came through it and a good many didn't, his friends and Hank's, and plenty they knew nothing about.

John wasn't about to get savage with him. Hank had his way of looking at it, and once they got across to Newfoundland, there was no chance they'd ever see each other again. There it was. Let Hank take it with him for the rest of his life, and he'd do the same.

Right now, it was back to base in Stephenville for Hank.

As for John and his plans, he didn't say anything. Hank didn't ask. He probably overheard them anyway, that night aboard the *Caribou.*

Just wished John good luck and held out his hand.

John accepted the handshake. Gave him some kind of smile, though not much of one. He hoped the Yank made out all right. He hoped the war didn't make a fuck of him, no more than he already was.

They all reached Port aux Basques none the worse for it. John hadn't been worried. He'd had it in his head that if the Germans showed up again and smacked them with another torpedo, then fuck them. That's what he was thinking, fuck them.

He'd have another go at staying alive. Not that he had a hope in hell of getting through it a second time. Of beating the odds a second time.

Port aux Basques and Channel, what most of the crew called home, was black as Hades, the both of them. Misery up and down every lane. Thirty-one crew drowned, fifteen left. Those who were from the place, when they got off the ship, could have been ghosts. It seemed hardly sensible to them that they were alive, when all their relatives had seen for days were dead bodies being lugged ashore.

John wasn't long there when he found out for certain that Miss Fitzpatrick was dead, her body found floating, lifebelt still on. Taken aboard a skiff and brought to Port aux Basques. It was sent by train to Bay Roberts. She would have wanted that, to be buried alongside her family.

And the Taverners then. The town buried the three of them, one after the other, the overcast sky and fog another shroud. There was no let-up. John stood back, inside the wrought-iron gate, dumbstruck and fitful, anxious to get away from the graveyard. He wanted to be on that train and find a way to drive those images behind him. He didn't say good-bye to Alex, only caught his eye and nodded. Then made for the station.

The military personnel had the railcar to themselves except for the civvy with the game leg. John was choking it down, the odd bugger out. Only a matter of time before he joined up. They somehow figured that. For now it was enough that the war had almost killed him.

Hank was in another railcar, but the G.I. was not aboard long, only as far as Stephenville Crossing. John called out to him standing on the platform with his buddies. 'Take it easy. Good bloody luck with the women.'

Then there was Charlotte to think about, and John did for a long time before going railcar to railcar in search of her. She was by herself, stiff as a cat in her seat by a window. Hands in white gloves in her lap, fingers locked together, eyes closed as if able to sleep.

John took the seat across from her. Clumsy as hell with his leg in that state. She stirred, dead set on not opening her eyes, her uniform, cleaned now but ragged, nothing close to what it was that night aboard the *Caribou*. She'd have a new one when she reached St. John's. Shoes to match.

Finally she got over it and half-opened her eyes. 'You can go now. I'm fine.'

John wasn't about to move.

Instead he said something about her saving his life.

She turned and stared out the window. Outside, the trees had turned yellow and red against the conifers.

'Most places in Newfoundland don't get fall colours as strong as that. Just the west coast of the island. Along the Humber River. Especially the Humber.'

She looked at him, but said nothing.

'The prairies neither?' he added.

There was no reason for her to care what he said.

He'd come visit when he got to St. John's, once the leg was better.

There was no figuring where her mind was. A cage with the door shut.

She'd be working. 'Come if you want.'

To judge by the way she put her gloved hand to her face, and then her neck, and back to her lap, she'd reached her limit.

John found a seat with a window to fill his time. He watched men on the river working logs that would eventually reach Bowater's newsprint mill in Corner Brook, huge booms of them. Odd. Odd to see lives that had nothing much to do with the war, nobody figuring they should be joining up.

It was torture getting off and on the train. He had to get some fresh air into him, get away from the tobacco smoke that hadn't slacked since they boarded.

One day there'd be a road from Deer Lake, up the peninsula to St. Anthony. He'd believe that when he saw it. A coastal boat from Lewisporte was all there was. Another five or six hours aboard the train. It was close to midnight when it finally pulled into Notre Dame Junction. Then the branch line to Lewisporte, and the wait for the coastal boat after that. Enough to try the patience of Job.

The patience of Job. Where had that come from? The past crawling back in.

Five days after starting out from Port aux Basques he was in St. Anthony, the good beat out of him, but home and alive.

He'd sent a telegram from Sydney to tell his mother he'd come through it. Nothing more until he got off the boat and hobbled his way to the house.

She laid eyes on her son, crutches holding him upright, and broke helplessly into tears. She held him fiercely, not emitting a word, quivering. Like she'd never again release him from her sight.

John hugged her back. But it wasn't him, not the fellow who left home to go aboard the *Caribou*.

When Sam showed up, John was stretched out on the daybed in the kitchen, spooning leftover pea soup and telling his mother only enough of what had happened to keep her mind from fraying any further.

'Hell, John.'

Sam pulled John's head into his chest. His eyes filled up, as though he was flesh and blood.

They'd been wracked with worry. A woman working with the Mission had an uncle who was an oiler aboard the *Caribou*. John wouldn't be the one to tell them, not about anyone cursed enough to have been in the engine room.

Sam rooted out of him what he could.

But John had had enough. He hadn't turned up home to have his mind returned to the Strait a dozen times over.

It came out that his leg bandage had been changed only once since he left the hospital in Port aux Basques. They insisted he go straight away to see Dr. Curtis. John had made a miserable job of it when he did change the bandage, and all that time sitting up had only made it worse.

Dr. Curtis had come from the States decades before, not long out of Harvard. When Grenfell retired and went to live in Vermont, the doctor took charge of the Mission.

Grenfell had died two years ago. John had often thought of him. His ashes were brought back and buried on Tea House Hill, behind the house where he and Mrs. Grenfell had lived with their children. John would hold off until his leg healed, but he'd make the trek up the hill and pay his respects.

Dr. Curtis was disgusted when he cut away the bandage, exposing a wound inflamed and seeping pus. As much as he was ready to, he didn't admonish the fellow, figuring John had gone through enough already. He cleaned the cut, disinfected it with iodine, then wrapped it with fresh bandage. It hurt something fierce. The price to be paid for not taking care of himself.

Before he left the hospital the doctor handed him a small bottle. Sulfonamide tablets. It would help clear the infection. John figured himself in better hands than he deserved.

His mother implored him to stay off his feet until the leg had a chance to heal. He slept when he could, when there wasn't a nightmare driving at him, when she wasn't stuffing him at the kitchen table.

Before he left home that first time, the trip he made to New York, he was bulked up, filled out soundly. Taller than Sam and more muscled. Sam took him on once for fun, and soon found out John could take care of himself when he had the mind to. When John returned home that spring, there was Sam, larger than life and married to his mother, a third person where there had only ever been two.

Sam took getting used to. His mother must have needed someone else in her life or she wouldn't have done it. That much he figured. As for himself—a fellow grows older. He works to get over it.

Or he leaves again. Sam was some of the reason, not all of it.

Sam had slipped into what should have been his father's place. Queer, John thought, what with Sam being his father's best friend. He could forgive Sam for that, if forgive was the right word. His mother had worked it out. He supposed he should be able to do the same. That he shouldn't have been getting on her nerves any more than he had already.

Then John back a week, practically back from the dead, and suddenly she had a lot to talk about, just the two of them in the kitchen. There was no place to get away from whatever was knocking about in her mind.

'Sit down. Have some tea. You're wound so tight.'

'I'm alive. Isn't that enough?'

'We were worried.'

We. So Sam had plenty to do with this sudden need to talk. No surprise there.

Sam went through a lot himself. John didn't need reminding, but he was fed-up with the questions. In his own good time he'd get past it. If they pushed him, it was not going to happen.

Sam showed up and right away knew what was going on. Something they planned, John figured. Sam poured himself a cup of tea and sat at the table across from him. Something John didn't need.

'Don't know how to say this...and I've put it off so long...do you want to know how your father died?'

Suddenly the golden opportunity.

All the times John had asked before, it was always the same until he gave up trying. John sat stiff and silent. Sam started in. Audience guaranteed.

He set up the story he had only ever hinted at before. It was early January 1916. He and Johnny were among the handful of men from the Newfoundland Regiment assigned to evacuate the last troops off the Gallipoli Peninsula. They worked like hell to trick the Turks into thinking there was nothing going on. They set fuses to blow sky high the dump of ammunition and equipment left on the beach. Everything timed to perfection.

That night 16,000 soldiers boarded lighters and got away. Not a single casualty. Only the evacuation party was left. Suddenly word reached them that a British general and his staff had been left stranded on a beach nearby when their boat ran aground. They would be trekking overland to join up with the others and make their escape.

Most of them showed up with time to spare. But not General Maude. He discovered his men had come away without his valise and kit and ordered them back to the boat to retrieve it. They started out a second time. Sam and Johnny were sent to look for them, with only minutes to spare before the beach was set to blow. They found the general, finally, huffing along, his valise broken open, papers flying everywhere, insisting that someone gather them up, the record of the shit campaign that was Gallipoli.

Johnny took him at his word. The classic soldier. Do or die. The poor bugger.

Sam's eyes were closed, failing to lessen the memory.

Sam figured he was right behind him. Figured when the lighter pushed away he would be there. That when the beach blew he would be sitting tight to him, the buddies they had always been.

That was it. Sam wiped his eyes and drank his tea. John left to say something.

His mother was sitting with them by then, her hand stretched out to cover her son's. No one spoke and when she patted his hand John drew it away and ran his fingers through his hair.

It made no difference. Except now there was a picture of how it happened where there was once only a vaguely imagined scene of his father slumped over the lip of a sniper's post.

John was suddenly deserving of the truth. The son was suddenly in need of a stiffer jolt to the consequences of war, more than what a German torpedo had done. War hadn't killed the son, but it did the job on the father. That was the message. That was a fact. Think how goddamn lucky you are, and get on with your life.

He told them he was joining up.

It was the perfect reply, perfectly timed.

There was no holding him back from proving he had a mind of his own, that he was more than the son and they had better learn how to deal with it.

Sam shook his head.

As if the step-father had any measure of control, as if he had any claim on where John's life was going.

'Why should you bloody care?'

Sam had heard it from John before. First when he showed up in St. Anthony. John had just finished school and was figuring out what he would do next. He told Sam he might join the Regiment. Sam turned on him. Said if he did enlist, he'd come looking for him and break every finger on both his goddamn hands. Droll as hell.

That was years ago. The First War had buggered him up. John knew where Sam's head was. He had laughed it off.

John was not about to brawl with him, not with his mother sitting next to them. He pushed away from the table and hobbled up the stairs.

Big surprise. There was a girl in the picture.

Eva, from Rhode Island. John noticed her every time he went to the hospital. She'd hurry about, doing all the things that keep Mission nurses busy. She was the one to lead him into the examining room, where he'd wait until Dr. Curtis turned up. The doctor was never on time and she'd keep coming back to check on Sam, even though he assured her he was perfectly okay.

She was not far off his height. A nest of reddish hair spread out from under her nurse's bonnet. An odd bit the way the bonnet banded tightly around the front of her head and fell down behind. The rest of her uniform, starched white, almost to the floor, but a snug fit. Or was it the fact she was younger than most Mission nurses, close to his own age if he guessed right.

The bonnet and the high-collar of her uniform framed her face, the pair of sunlit blue eyes. At first glance, mismatched for her hair colour, but different, full of life, inviting. With a smile she seemed to be holding in check. He kept stealing glances.

The doctor came in that first time and told him to let down his trousers so he could have a look at the leg. John unfastened his belt, glanced at Eva, and worked his trousers to his knees. Her eyes fixed on the bandage and not on him.

He figured she was secretly keen on seeing him that way. The sight of bare flesh, when she was so bound up in all that uniform.

He never knew a nurse to be shy. They couldn't do their job if they were.

Eva had been in St. Anthony a few months by then. She'd settled in, though it was no Providence, Rhode Island. She was kept too busy to think about it. Dr. Curtis expected a lot of her, as he did of everyone who ever worked for him. She liked it, liked having plenty to do.

Liked being part of the Mission. She'd met Dr. Grenfell once, when she was a young girl. Her Aunt Jessie knew him. Which made Eva special because everyone, John's mother included, thought the world of Jessie Luther and how she had devoted herself to the Mission in its early days. The talk was that Jessie Luther was keen on Dr. Grenfell before he up and married a well-to-do young woman from Chicago. All water under the bridge now.

So Eva came with a history. Connections were made to her past, all good reason to talk more, get to know her better. This time, after the doctor left the room and she handed John his crutches, he asked her straight out if she would walk with him sometime, when he tried it without the crutches. Like it could be taken as medical work, part of her job, if she were to look at it that way.

She said she would. It was the first time he was stirred up since he'd arrived home.

That Sunday afternoon he showed up at Grenfell House. Soon after the Grenfells moved to Vermont, the house was changed into a residence for hospital staff. John had been there once before, as a kid with his mother. She ran the Mission's handicrafts store, and she'd gone to deliver a bundle of hooked mats to Mrs. Grenfell, for her approval. He had stayed in the hallway, sneaking a glimpse of the white polar bear skin rug splayed on the floor in the parlour. In a boy's mind Grenfell House was forbidden luxury. People in St. Anthony still called it *The Castle*.

He had arranged with Eva to show up at three. He did so determined to prove it was no trouble to climb the steps onto the veranda, on the chance someone was watching through a window. There was a rank of tall windows, for the sunroom that surrounded the house on two sides.

The housekeeper who answered his knock called it the conservatory. She asked if he would like to take one of its several seats. He was expected. She would tell Eva he was there, in the conservatory. She called her Miss Eva.

He smiled and passed on greetings from his mother.

She stopped and looked at him and told him it was good to see him looking so well. After all the torment he had gone through.

His story had arrived ahead of him. He wasn't surprised.

Dr. Grenfell was always keen on the healing power of sunlight. Patients bundled up in wheelchairs was a common sight on the veranda of the hospital. The conservatory promised the same. A place to take to a Morris chair with a book, racks of caribou antlers perched on the walls overhead. Hooked rugs scattered about the painted hardwood floor, small side tables for tea. And, with any luck, sunshine.

No one could ever count on sunshine, not in St. Anthony. And not that day.

'It could very well rain,' according to Eva. 'Are you sure you want to go?'

He thought to say that he was used to water, but he held off and chuckled then. It helped.

He set off, the cocky fellow out to show the young woman from Rhode Island there was no need to worry. He'd already gone a couple of days without the crutches.

His leg well oiled. Right as rain.

Her plan was to take the trail along Tea House Hill, to where the Grenfell ashes were entombed.

Jim dandy. He smiled once more.

It was frosty and fresh, crisp under foot, a fall day intensified by Eva. No rain. A downpour of snowflakes if anything.

Except the trail turned steeper in places, more so than he remembered. Trekking uphill put new pressure on his leg. He muzzled the pain and gritted his way through without Eva noticing. As he hoped.

She suggested they sit awhile when they came to a level spot and a bench.

'I'm fine. But we can if you wish.'

She wasn't fooled.

'Are you happy coming north, despite the weather?' There were no leaves left on the trees.

'More to life than weather.'

It was a minefield. And she was persistent.

The ferry, the job, everything he could think of that wasn't about the night it happened.

He shrugged it off, his lame smile no help.

She understood. But maybe he did need to talk about it. Maybe he'd feel better.

She didn't understand.

He tried hard not to mess it up more. He got her moving again. Slower this time. Time enough to work through the torment coming through his leg.

They made it to the bronze plaques, one each for Dr. Grenfell and his wife, Anne, attached to the broad face of a boulder, pockmarked by black and orange lichens. The plaques were bolted over places in the rock face that had been hollowed out to hold the urns. Eva brushed her mittened hand over one of them.

Wilfred Thomason Grenfell. 1865-1940. Life is a Field of Honour.

John worked it out, the field of honour.

She reached for his bare hand and held it between both of hers, warming it with her mittens.

He thought he would have felt more. What he felt was bothered. Grudging that it hadn't gone better. That he wasn't wrapping himself in her like he'd had the urge to do for weeks. He wanted something more. He wanted to pitch the rest behind him and get on with it.

Walking the trail up the hill had been troublesome. Walking back down was worse. By the time they reached Grenfell House the leg was giving him hell.

She insisted he come inside and rest.

He had lost patience, told her good-bye and hobbled off, thinking he looked and sounded like a fool. Pity was the last thing he was about to handle.

At home he didn't say enough to rile them. They had nothing to complain about. The leg had its rest, and this time he stayed off it. It got better in its own good time.

Dr. Curtis gave him another once over and that was the end of the visits. John handed over the crutches and walked home. He and Eva didn't have a lot to say to each other, but there it was, over and done with.

Then a note arrived from Grenfell House, inviting him to dinner. It could only have been Eva who added his name.

He was playing a different tune. He was a fellow with a lot more rooting around in his head.

Just because a chunk of him was bruised and battered didn't mean it wasn't on his mind more than ever it was. The tap hadn't been shut. It still drove him crazy, a fellow wanted it so bad sometimes.

He didn't want to be looking at her only that way, but Eva was his best chance. Even if they didn't have much in common.

She said she wanted to apologize, when they were finally alone after dinner.

He told her there was nothing to apologize for.

She called it presumptuous. Trying to help. That it was not anything she should have been doing.

It was not anything he wanted to be talking about.

She looked around, not at him as he stood next to her in the side room that had once been Dr. Grenfell's office, which still had the doctor's heavy, roll-top desk filling most of the space.

Forget everything, he told her.

He stared at her until she looked at him again. Into each other's eyes, until it was not what she knew of him before, him naked of his storyline. Into her eyes where he knew how to lose himself in their landscape. He wanted only himself and Eva, bare of their pasts, surrendered.

He drew closer to her, and drew her closer to him. She resisted, but only for the moment it took to press his lips more expectantly against hers, her body pressed against a bookcase.

The kiss burned, his caution lurched away.

There was no mistaking where it was leading and no holding back until she pressed her hands against his chest and tried to push him away. He felt the ridges of her fists.

He drew back. He said nothing.

She didn't admonish him as he anticipated. She was waiting for an apology.

She told him he needed to know her. She straightened her dress.

He wanted to.

She didn't believe him.

That night, despite her doubts, they slipped up two flights of stairs unseen and into her bedroom and locked the door. He was too anxious to think about the reason, assured her he had what they needed for protection.

In the dark he tugged free of his clothes. She removed hers slowly, setting each piece aside.

She opened herself to him and there was no thought of anything but a quickened passage into her. He burst before there was time to relish it.

He fell to one side of her and she turned toward the other. She covered the both of them with a quilt. He drew tight to her back and held her against him. She took his hand and placed it against her breasts. He kissed her neck , buried his face in it. She had stopped shaking.

He went to see Eva the next evening. He walked to Grenfell House and they sat in the conservatory. It should have been easier, but the gap between them had widened. He didn't understand it.

He pushed ahead blindly. Invited her to go snowshoeing that Sunday afternoon.

She thought not.

He kept at it, and eventually she gave in. He could see no reason not to. They needed time.

On Sunday they took a level trail that ran through the woods to the edge of a pond where they lit a fire. He broke some dry spruce boughs and piled them up, then set the snowshoes on top as a place for them to sit. It was not particularly comfortable, but the fire helped and in his knapsack he had everything needed to make tea. Something he had done dozens of times before.

'In Newfoundland no one ever goes in the woods without stopping to make tea.'

She found in his attempt to educate her to the island's customs a reason to smile. He positioned a stick over the fire and hung the kettle from it. They drank their tea from enamel mugs and ate a slice each of his mother's bread, spread with partridgeberry jam.

But when the ritual had passed, the knapsack repacked and set aside, and he attempted to take her hand, she found reason to keep it from him. When he thought to kiss her she resisted.

She wasn't giving him a chance.

'I made a mistake,' she told him.

'That sounds like an excuse.'

'I'm happy in St. Anthony. You're anxious to leave.'

She was discovering his country. He was tired of it. He was desperate for something. Something more than sex.

He had trouble saying the word.

It had summed him up, a word pulled through muddled air.

He wasn't letting go. He wanted her to look at him. A simple request. It wasn't mindless. Please.

She turned to him reluctantly.

He was not what she took him for. Apparently her answer.

He couldn't just will himself free of what happened. His answer.

That and time.

Ah, Paris. u-boat commanders live for Paris, our city of enlightenment, *absolument*.

Above all, the Shéhérazade, a glamour pit on rue de Liège where a commander is welcomed with arms wide open, where he loses himself deliciously in wine and women and Russian waltzes. Less devoted sons have been known to forego their furloughs home in favour of extended respites with ladies they have come to know at the Shéhérazade.

In my few days in Paris I also came to know such a lady, but in my case there were obstacles to outdistance, my thoughts of Elise foremost among them. And, as much as she gallantly tried, it became clear that Yvette—the dark-eyed, angelic Yvette, with whom I was sharing the Piper Heidsieck—was heartsore. There had been an officer in her life who had not returned from his last patrol. I like to think our chatter helped ease her distress, but that was not, after all, what I had arrived at the Shéhérazade to do. I lost myself to the champagne instead.

The nightclub and restaurant were the creation of Vladimir, a White Russian who escaped St. Petersburg in the wake of the Bolsheviks. It was an outpost for Russians in Paris, but, as it turned out, equally one for u-boat officers and the staff of command headquarters. Even Dönitz was known to show up from time to time.

To a Dresden boy the Shéhérazade was supremely exotic. Walls and ceilings draped with fringed and tasseled Arabian fabrics, striped deep red, purple, and gold, lit by brass lanterns embedded with mosaics of coloured crystals. Tables spread with intricately patterned silver—jugs and ashtrays, vases of fresh flowers, urns of champagne.

And under that fragmented lighting were told the stories of its U-boat men, commanders who, like me, had set out in frigid seas, not knowing what, if any, enemy vessels would cross their paths. Who, by grit and chance, would return triumphant, or, at the least, rewarded with an extension of their count. And who had no end of reason to celebrate. For they were alive and men who had celebrated with them before were not.

I sought him out—Erich Topp. One of our top dogs, who sent thirty-five vessels to their graves, reassigned now to a new job, no longer leading patrols. He had taken charge of the U-boat training flotilla in the Baltic.

Topp has not been the same since the loss of Endrass, his soul mate, another captain from Crew 34. Herr Hitler presented Engelbert Endrass with Oak Leaves for his Knight's Cross in June of '41. In October he left for his tenth patrol and was never heard from again.

Topp and Endrass were thick as thieves, inseparable friends, separated forever by the freakish whim of war. Their comrades called them Castor and Pollux, the twin brothers of Greek mythology. Topp lived to eclipse his friend. A pair of Crossed Swords was added to his Oak Leaves.

Topp was on a short respite from the Baltic. When I laid eyes on him, he was seated at a quiet corner table, no longer the bon viveur he was when he and Endrass came together to the Shéhérazade.

He was sitting with a young woman, a Russian dancer whom I had seen perform at the club the night before. She was not in costume and appeared to be there solely to spend the evening with Topp. There was a third, a woman whom I took to be a friend of Endrass. They looked a melancholy threesome.

I hesitated approaching him, even though we had been introduced somewhere along the way, by Teddy Suhren. Topp knew him well.

'Gräf, yes, I remember now. Teddy spoke highly of you.'

I wasn't sure I believed him.

'I leave again on the second, from Lorient.'

'Teddy has been reassigned you know. Also to U-boat training.'

I nodded. I was well aware of that. The aces had done their duty. Considered too valuable to risk any longer. It left the late-comers to take their chances.

'Any advice?'

It was an awkward way of stating it, and I could see I had overstepped my welcome. He would rather not have been discussing business, so to speak.

'I'll leave you to it, *Korvettenkapitän*.' I nodded slightly. 'Ladies.' I nodded again. 'Enjoy your evening.'

'Gräf, what is it?'

'You had a stellar reputation among your men, Topp. They would have followed you to the ends of the earth.'

He thought for a moment. 'Get to know them, Gräf. You will not like them all, but know their stories, how they came to be aboard your boat, know the families they left behind.'

It was something I prided myself on already.

'And Gräf, do your best to hide your deficiencies. We all have them, whether we admit it or not.'

'Good evening, Topp.' I drew away from them and back to where I had been sitting. Yvette's mood had not improved.

Deficiencies—according to the Naval Academy we had none. And we were not long into the war when men like Prien and Schepke, like Topp and Endrass, only confirmed that was the case, even though they were on the prowl during the height of the Happy Time, practically sinking ships at will.

I would come to admit these high liners had a greater flair for the job, even if all but Topp had their savvy at the helm catch up to them. Each of the other three had gone to the bottom at the height of their game.

Deficiencies then, we all have them. Patience. I suspect I don't have the patience of Topp. Confidence. His dozen patrols proved a boost no doubt.

I escorted Yvette to a larger table and surrounded myself with other commanders of a similar rawness. I needed their bluster. I was not about to have my nights in Paris turn morose.

The champagne enabled the catharsis, as did the cognac. We caroused the night away, not once compromising the dignity of the place. Even our renditions of *Das kann doch einen Seemann nicht erschüttern* had an air of courtliness. Dönitz would have been proud.

Yvette proved a distraction, little more. I had gained no interest in an amorous interlude, which surprised her I suppose. It being Paris, there being glitter still despite the war, a man would expect more of himself, more audacity as we exited the taxi and I walked her to the door of her apartment.

There was a light sprinkle of snow, enough to further charm the night as it fell on the shoulders and hood of her cape. She had the most inviting lips. She asked me inside. I hesitated, lacking the élan of a commander.

'You're thinking of her. That's admirable. I don't often see it.'

I kissed her gently on the lips and left it at that. I suspect she was relieved as much as anything. She was far from over her loss, and I would have done nothing to help her past it. Nor would she have done anything but arouse my guilt. We parted friends. And with the promise of seeing each other the next time I was in Paris.

It was into November and the *Baccalieu* was about to make what might be her last run for the season. If winter set in, if fresh ice crowded the harbour, then the only way out of St. Anthony would be overland by dog team. A pounding trip across scabrous terrain that John could never handle. As it was he should have given the leg more time. When the coastal boat pulled into the government wharf and cast ashore her lines, John was packed and chafing to go.

His mother had suffered through his unspoken eagerness to get away. She urged him to stay, until spring at least. She was certain the Mission would find him a job.

He'd said nothing more about joining up, but she could tell it had rooted in his mind. Why else would he be heading to St. John's?

As for Sam, he didn't threaten a second time to break his fingers.

The day came, and what few words they exchanged circled around his promise to write. Her voice breaking, her expectations struggling to hold.

John embraced her, then pressed himself away from them and turned toward the vessel. Her gaze followed him up the gang-plank, minding the slight falter in his step. He stood for a while at the railing and looked back at them, until it grew awkward not calling back and forth as the other newly boarded passengers were doing. He disappeared inside, returning to the railing when the hawsers were loosened and pulled aboard the ship. He held up his hand until his mother and Sam were distant enough that he could comfortably walk away.

St. John's was a city reshaped by the incongruities of war. As Germans stiff-marched into Poland, Newfoundland cobbled together a militia to defend its capital city. With reports of an enemy U-boat fleet poised to slink across the ocean, it strung an anti-submarine net across the mouth of its harbour. It rezoned its cityscape in anticipation of the swarms of allied troops about to entrench themselves ashore.

It was clear that St. John's needed to dramatically safeguard its war footing. Within months, Canadian Army troops descended on the city. Reinforced concrete batteries were erected on opposite sides of the harbour and implanted with fast-action artillery and sweeping searchlights. At Cape Spear rose a counter-bombardment battery with a fearsome pair of ten-inch guns. Anti-aircraft batteries were set up at the airport in Torbay, on the Hill O' Chips, and across the harbour in the South Side Hills. An internment camp for potential prisons of war took shape overnight on the shores of Quidi Vidi Lake. Now, when Hitler lusted across the Atlantic he'd see a cocky little bastion set to do its ruddy best.

The Canadian Army was soon joined by its Air Force and Navy. And in January of 1941, a troop ship carrying a thousand of the U.S. Army's finest docked in the harbour. Within months they took up permanent residence in the 200 freshly constructed buildings of what they named Fort Pepperrell. Thousands more G.I.s followed.

The centuries-old fish port of St. John's was suddenly a burgeoning military outpost, replete with tent cities, parade squares, and dance halls. Army vehicles jostled through cobblestone streets. Foreign flags fluttered where only the Union Jack had flown before. Thousands of the city's young women were about to have the time of their lives.

John departed the train station on Water Street, his hopes high. The Red Triangle, the YMCA hostel, was a short distance away. It would be for a few nights only, until the papers were signed and he was on his way overseas. He had stayed in a YMCA in New York years before and remembered it with some fondness.

He was hardly through the main entrance when his heart sank. The reception area was thick with servicemen, standing about, smoking, jabbering on. Louder, boisterous chatter streamed from a large open area beyond, what looked to be a bar and social club. John turned to a pert young lady ensconced behind a broad desk. She smiled indulgently. The facility was strictly for the use of Canadian Forces personnel. There was nothing she could do for him. She wished him luck, swivelled her office chair and resumed her chitchat with a trio of brassy young officers clustered nearby.

He did no better at the Caribou Hut. John had known the hulk of a brick building at the opposite end of Water Street to be the Seaman's Institute, a refuge for outport men and women new to the city, set up by none other than Wilfred Grenfell, a man he had surely counted among his friends. But the war had turned it into another hostel for the military. John was set back on the street again.

He tried the Knights of Columbus hostel on Harvey Road. He argued in vain that give him a day or two and he'd be a military man as slick as any of them. Another blank, patronizing stare.

He ended up in an overcrowded boarding house on Cabot Street, sharing a room with some fellow from Carbonear, in the city to work construction on the American base. He managed a way past his snoring and woke early the next morning with his hopes reset.

He went in search of the RAF enlistment station. It was not to be found. Recruitment for the RAF was at a standstill. Since the war started, a few hundred Newfoundlanders had been accepted for training as air and ground crews, but the number who would likely pass the stringent examinations had dwindled. Quotas were not being met. It was no longer worth the recruitment effort. Better he try the navy.

He did, grudgingly. The Royal Navy, too, had halted recruitment. With the Allied landings in North Africa, there were no troop ships to be spared to transport men across the Atlantic. As it was, there were barely enough ships to carry the food supplies needed to keep Britain from starvation. Better he find passage to England and try his luck there.

That would prove his one hope—passage to England aboard one of the merchant vessels that were regularly part of the convoys that left North America for Britain, setting out from St. John's with cargoes of dried codfish and mail.

He landed on the doorstep of Furness Withy.

The company had one ship due to join a convoy. Later in December, most likely. Sometime after Christmas. The *Tudor Prince* with a load of fish, and looking for a few more crewmen with merchant ship experience.

That he had, John told him, although the fellow wasn't so sure, until John made it known he was someone who had survived the *Caribou*. That commanded notice. The fellow slipped to a back room and returned with someone taller, better dressed, who had more authority than he did. In his hand was a folded piece of newspaper, a survivor list published in *The Daily News*. Plain for all to see: John Gilbert, steward.

He got a job, without letting on he had no intention of taking the voyage back.

When he did set foot in Newfoundland again it would be in uniform, the war under his belt.

He resigned to his boarding house. He would put up with it for a couple of weeks. Give his leg more rest. Give him the opportunity to search out Charlotte.

He was back to himself now. As far as she would be able to tell.

The woman he found at the Canadian Navy Hospital on Forest Road smiled liberally at seeing how well he had recovered. She herself had needed time, had only recently returned to her regular shift at the hospital.

Her day-to-day work reclaimed her. She had stolen a few moments away from the wards, though she was anxious he not prolong the visit. She sat at the edge of the padded bench that ran against one wall of the waiting room. Her questions sprang from one to the other, as did her answers.

She kept a close eye on the watch clipped to the pocket of her pristine uniform. When she did stand up to return to work it was with purposeful energy. He asked if he would see her again. She made no commitment, though neither did she refuse. She headed to the wards, his hope left to work itself out.

Charlotte had arrived back in St. John's in a state of near collapse. Unknown to John and most others on the train, she had accompanied the body of her friend. Martha had been assistant matron at the hospital and her drowning struck a deep blow to all who knew her. She was buried with naval honours at the Canadian military cemetery in the city.

Charlotte had come through her ordeal only with the staunch attention of the other Nursing Sisters. Their devotion to her recovery made them wary of anything that might provoke a relapse. They looked on John with doubt.

He was at a disadvantage from the start, there being such an abundance of military men stationed in the city. There was not a day that went by that Charlotte didn't encounter someone who would have asked her out at the drop of a hat had she not put them off before the conversation reached that awkward moment.

It was only a matter of time. She came to feel the need for someone new in her life, someone who wouldn't have known what she had been through. There was an RCAF lieutenant from Victoria who was particularly persistent.

Chance had brought John to the periphery of Charlotte's life. It had implanted excessive emotion in his memories. But it was best if it stopped at that. It was not in her to be anything but generous, yet her intention was to discourage the young man, to let him down gently.

John remained impulsively hopeful.

For starters, they could stroll along Duckworth and Water streets and take in the stores decorated for Christmas. Or take in a dance. From what he gathered, there were plenty of them catering to the military, and she could certainly take him as her guest.

On December 12, John stood with hundreds more on Harvey Road and watched as fire engulfed the Knights of Columbus

Hostel and burnt it to a pile of cinders. He had been sitting behind blackout curtains, he and three other boarders, drinking cheap Jamaican rum and listening to Uncle Tim's Barn Dance on VOCM, broadcast live from the Hostel.

They had jabbered through singer Biddy O'Toole's rendition of "My Bonnie Boy in Blue." It was all too maudlin for single men with no foreseeable prospects of women. They took to Teddy Adams singing "The Moonlight Trail" a bit more, but partway through the song the music stopped abruptly.

Screams rang out and someone could be heard shouting a warning of fire. There was a weak attempt to restart the music. Suddenly the radio broadcast went dead.

The men looked at each other, then rushed to the hallway and into winter coats and boots. They were outside in seconds, running and skidding along the icy roads to the hostel, joined by dozens of others who had rushed out from other houses. The sky ahead of them glowed red.

John's first thought was of Charlotte, of the likelihood of her being inside. Of her having gone to the dance with some Yank in uniform.

On Harvey Road they discovered the worst. Flames and smoke were shooting from upstairs windows. Fire had burst through the roof. Before their eyes the fire spread downstairs and into the dance hall. Within minutes the hostel was a ball of flame. Anyone inside who had not managed to escape would never do so.

John stood motionless, stunned. The impotence consumed him, forcing him to some edge he thought he had escaped. Then he caught sight of her. Held upright by a fellow in uniform as dishevelled as herself, greyed by smoke and soot, coughing through a hand pressed to her mouth. The fellow lifted her in his arms and walked away. She had survived a second time.

It was the last John saw of her. Charlotte and her officer were two of the many who escaped the fire. Ninety-nine more did not.

The catastrophe bred rumours. That the fire had been set by a German spy set ashore in Newfoundland by one of their U-boats, the same one that sank the *Caribou,* or that struck the ore carriers docked at Bell Island. In a city rife with military men, some imposter in a pilfered uniform would have gone unnoticed. There were other suspicious fires—at the Shamrock Field barracks and the Old Colony Club—that were contained, but further fed the rumours.

It left the city on edge. It took the good out of Christmas. The store windows along Water Street lost their magic. Midnight Mass opened with prayers for those who had fallen to the flames and the many in hospital recovering from their burns. Christmas Day dinners carried an air of solemnity and guilt.

The city only returned to itself as snow fell over the charred ruins on Harvey Road, and convoy crews reached port with stories of more ships torpedoed by German U-boats. This time it was two cargo steamships that had gone to the bottom, everyone aboard lost. When the first torpedo struck, forty merchant navy men of the *Montreal City* had taken to lifeboats, not to be heard from again.

When John left port on the 3rd of January he fortified himself against the menace that likely lay ahead. The *Tudor Prince* was destined for Liverpool. The expectation was for a treacherous crossing.

At 0800 the following day the *Tudor Prince* was the last ship to join Convoy HX 221 that had started in New York on the 29th, with ships from Halifax added on January 1. There were now thirty-eight in all, escorted by seven ships of the British and Canadian navies—five corvettes and two destroyers. The convoy was led by Commodore B.B. Grant of the Royal Naval Reserve, aboard a Norwegian merchant vessel bound for Glasgow, the *Abraham Lincoln.*

On his previous assignment—HX 212 in October—Grant had served as Vice-Commodore, aboard the same ship. That crossing had been a disaster—seven vessels torpedoed, close to 300 men lost.

Grant envisaged rough weather, something to play havoc with the U-boats. For two days he was granted his wish. He wrote in his log: *heavy sea and swell, overcast with sleet and snow, visibility mainly poor.* The visibility improved after that, though the heavy sea and swell held until the 9th. A couple of days later it picked up again.

There was an additional factor in his favour. A month earlier the British, using intelligence salvaged from a U-boat that had foundered off Port Said, had broken the code of the latest version of Enigma, the enciphering machine perfected by the Germans. Once again the British were able to pinpoint the positions of the Dönitz's wolfpacks hunting the North Atlantic. On the same day that the *Tudor Prince* joined HX 221, Grant received amended routing instructions from the convoy's navigator and set the ships on a new course.

John knew nothing of this. His mind was fixed on carrying out his duties as steward despite the roll and pitch of the *Tudor Prince.* At a length of just over 300 feet, a GRT of 1900 tons, and a crew of forty men, the vessel was nothing compared to the *Caribou.* His job had shrunk to something makeshift.

He had barely settled aboard ship when the chief steward called him up and outlined his duties. The man had crossed the Atlantic a dozen times since the war began. He stood for nothing but the way he ordered things done.

John's main responsibility would be the food—managing the stores, keeping track of what was on the shelves and what had been used. Seeing that the men were fed on time, in a descent fashion. Keeping the meal stations clean. Above all, he was warned, maintaining hygiene. If careless handling of food spread dysentery through the crew, there would be hell to pay.

John buckled down to it and the turmoil of the seas outside went largely unnoticed. His time aboard the *Caribou* had given him a sound pair of sea legs. Only when he navigated his way from below deck to deliver food and drink to those manning the bridge did he come face to face with the ferocity of the North Atlantic in winter. Wind and sleet pounded the convoy, which nevertheless made steady headway.

The men on watch duty were content with what they faced. It was obvious that no U-boats, even if there were any in the vicinity, were about to attack in such seas. They would have to resurface at some point to recharge their batteries, but it wouldn't be to prowl about, setting sights on the convoy.

His visits to the bridge quickly turned to the best part of his job. It set the lowly steward in the midst of the ship's unrelenting advance. He developed an alliance with the men on watch duty, enough that from time to time he was handed an extra pair of binoculars. He quickly learned to identify the ships that surrounded them.

The vessels held in columns, five hundred yards between them, a thousand yards column to column. They often changed position, some experiencing mechanical trouble, not able to keep up the pace Commodore Grant had set. These stragglers were left to make out as best they could. Grant certainly wasn't willing to slow the convoy in deference to them. They'd set their engine room crews to work in frantic attempts to make repairs in time enough to rejoin the convoy.

One ship in particular caught his attention, one even smaller than their own, by some forty feet he estimated. The *Zamalek*. A rescue ship. Assigned to convoys to take aboard survivors from ships sunk by German torpedoes.

John had never heard of such a vessel. The rescue ships, he was told, were a haphazard collection, repurposed coastal-cargo and passenger ships, requisitioned by the British Admiralty after the huge losses during the Atlantic crossings in the early months of the war. Rescue ships had a lower freeboard than most, to make rescue easier, and more storage area for food and water, and room to quarter survivors, if they could get to them.

Not all convoys were fortunate enough to have a rescue ship. And the *Zamalek* had the reputation of being the best of the lot. She had saved some 350 men who would otherwise have perished in the frigid waters.

The ship had the same master since she went into service, a Captain Morris, and much of the same crew, men like Morris who had remained fiercely loyal despite the constant danger. Her sister ship, also a rescue ship, the *Zaafaran,* had been sunk, and it was the *Zamalek* who had rescued her crew and the survivors she had aboard at the time.

The rescue ships were based out of Glasgow, and it was to there that the *Zamalek* was returning after her trip out with convoy ON 151, and now back again with HX 221.

It proved to be an uneventful trip for the *Zamalek,* as it was for the *Tudor Prince*. The convoy struck rough weather again on the 11th, by which time the *Tudor Prince* and five more vessels had detached under escort from the convoy and made for Liverpool.

By the 13th, the weather fine and clear, the *Zamalek,* along with the other ships destined for Glasgow, split from the convoy, her assignment complete.

A little over two weeks later, on February 2, 1943, attached to convoy ON 165, the *Zamalek* would head out from Glasgow again, destined for St. John's. Newfoundland. Aboard was the newest member of the crew, a man who had grown up in Newfoundland, who had turned up in Glasglow determined to convince Captain Morris to take him aboard. He called himself Johnny Gilbert.

I ARRIVED BACK IN LORIENT ON THE 29TH, AFTER A TEDIOUS rail journey in which I retreated into a clandestine copy of Rilke for most of the way, then went directly to Elise. Her visit with her parents in Munich had gone much better than mine to Dresden. Her holiday had refreshed her, though her train trip back, like mine, had been disrupted several times. Rail travel these days is grim torment.

We fell into each other's arms at the first private moment. I had a few days only before I was due to re-board U-69.

My eagerness was unequivocal.

It unsettled her to think our relationship was suddenly constricted, as if we dared not think beyond that stretch of time. I was being practical. I boldly asserted we loved each other more than anyone else in the world. It could be glorious if we gave into it, surrendered ourselves to all it was worth.

But our love-making bore little of the freedom it had known before. She tried, but it was not the same.

Strangely, it was the aftermath that marked us the most. We were cocooned beneath thick blankets, our barrier against the winter outside, her breasts against my back, her lower body curved into mine. With her free hand she slowly stroked my chest. She nuzzled her face into my neck.

When I turned onto my back, she whispered in my ear. 'I'm afraid for you, Ulrich,' all the time her hand caressing my chest.

She needed reassurance that nothing would come of my return to sea, that in six weeks, as before, we would be wrapped in each other again.

She cried, but said nothing more. And when we dressed, and returned to the world outside ourselves, I sensed a further distance, an unwillingness to look into my eyes without turning away and filling the gap with mindless chatter. As if she were afraid of it filling up with gloom.

She was not herself, and then suddenly bitter. 'A needless war,' she said, sitting next to me in the open air of the town square.

I found myself defending it, as if in doing so it would ease the torment.

'The Nazis,' she flung back at me, 'what do they know?'

Her irreverence, infused with anger, widened the gap between us. Yet, if I were truthful, my misgivings were equal to her own. In frustration, I said as much. 'There'll be an end to it. One way or another.'

True of every war, of course, but just what that end would be seemed to grow increasingly uncertain. It was impossible to ignore the mistrust that Elise had uttered, for there was a steady undertow of skepticism, if rarely allowed a voice. Elise was being reckless, and my look cautioned her to keep her thoughts between us.

All this for the sake of love.

It was not how it should have been, the time we had, fragmented as it was, both of us with other commitments. I was resolute in not leaving Lorient moody and ungratified.

I held her hand in the pocket of my trench coat as we walked the deserted beach in Larmor-Plage. The sand was stiff with frost and the ocean lapped to shore without the eagerness it did when we had come the month before. *L'Hôtel du Lapin Blanc* was closed until spring and when the chill off the water was too much, we huddled together on the steps of its veranda, our view across the channel to the lighthouse at Port-Louis. The day was dull and windless, the lighthouse dormant, now that the submarine bunkers at Lorient had become nighttime targets for the RAF. Our trip to the beach seemed but a vain attempt to recapture the magic of our summer visit.

What we had was each other. The isolation forced us momentarily closer, forced us to find refuge in what we did have at that moment, pushing aside what was unknowable.

We made no mention of it after that, instead choosing the next night to soundly cheer in the New Year. I had convinced Elise to celebrate in the officer's club, a place she had never been despite being asked several times, so she said. I sported my superior powers of persuasion. It made her laugh and, when the time came, eased our public exposure as a couple.

Our entrance caused a momentary breach in the conversations, and it was suddenly obvious that Elise was a prize that had been denied a number of men in the room. I relished it, for up to the point at least, I was far from the most noteworthy officer among them. It was just the beginning.

I had no idea what Elise had chosen to wear until I helped her out of her standard nursing overcoat. My eyes widened, falling on a dark purple lace gown, sprinkled with sequins, a neckline cut to the edge of her cleavage. I folded the overcoat and hung it on my arm. My breathing resumed.

The gown clung to her in so many exceptional ways, down to her knees, where it flared out, to slightly above a pair of open-toed heels. The lace sleeves ended just shy of her wrists, one bordering a gold filigree bracelet.

I stood, still holding up the overcoat, motionless for the moment. She looked stunning, about to charm the evening in ways

I had not imagined. As we settled into a table, somewhere in the middle distance between the bar and the stage, we gathered even more envy. I feigned indifference.

I played out the evening for all its suavity. Champagne it would be. When the young lady came to our table and stood between us, we ordered a bottle in Elise's best French. The effort pleased her and when she returned with the bottle in an ice bucket, suitably robed in a white linen towel, she made something of an elaborate display of uncorking the bottle and filling our long stemmed glasses. I proposed a toast, whispered in Elise's ear.

'To us. To love. To a future together. *Prosit Neujahr!*'

It was with all the intimate exuberance I could summon. Even that was a risk. I feared Elise would find it facile, superficial, more denial of the days ahead.

But she played her part wonderfully well. We ate smoked salmon and caviar and nonchalantly added to the conversations circling the tables. We took to the dance floor and did the rumba, ineptly on my part to be sure, but I defiantly pressed on, following her lead, half-drunk by then. The musicians loved it. The Kernével buffoons standing at the bar glared our way as if we were an insult to the navy.

At the stroke of midnight, we kissed, as passionately as we dared in public.

'*Frohes neues Jahr!*'

One of the buffoons forced himself between us, swung Elise away from me, and kissed her on the lips. '*Frohes neues Jahr!*' he exclaimed again, and presented her back to me.

I pushed my open palm into his face and drove him back. The swine stumbled, more out of surprise than from the force.

Already other officers were between us, holding us back.

'Gräf,' said the fellow who had a grip on me, 'it's New Year's! He was having fun.'

The others taunted me, their liquor stirring a surge of laughter. I was suddenly the bad sport. They expected me to withdraw, crowding around me and slapping me on the back. The bastard returned to the bar, something of a victor.

Elise, in an attempt to cover her embarrassment, had returned to the table. I fell into the chair beside her.

'Ulrich, you're drunk.'

It was meant to excuse me.

'The bastard.'

I held back from adding to the clutter of the situation. Her silence eased and she pressed her hand against mine. I edged closer to her. My vision wavered, coming to dwell on the curve of her neck, on how perfect it was, and had I not retained a bit of judgment, I would have kissed her there.

'Don't brood,' she said. 'Don't waste the time.'

I was too glazed to have any thoughts other than kissing her. That would fill all the time in the world.

In the revelry of the next song she retrieved her overcoat and, routing us away from the bar, led the way outside.

It was snowing heavily. We huddled together, in something of what was surely a winter wonderland, though in the darkness we could only imagine it, except for the feathery flakes that drifted directly down on us. Then, in the centre of Lorient, scattered thin tongues of fireworks erupted, one trailing away before another followed lamely after it. It was a tentative gesture of defiance by a few Frenchmen determined to outlast their invaders.

Suddenly, it was a call to arms. The RAF emerged unseen, the unmistakable grinding roar of enemy aircraft rising in the distance. The pair lashed their bombs at the U-boat bunkers, the explosions a massive counterpoint to the paltry fireworks.

The bombs fell to no avail, of course, as they had done before, the thick bunkers doing the job expected of them. I watched with drunken conceit. If I knew better, I was not to admit it.

Elise and I huddled together, the snow falling to earth around us, until the bombers disappeared. We had each other, tightly bound against any suspicions.

We never before made love with such hope, with such desperation. We seethed with it, her nakedness filling every fraction of my mind. I ended deep inside her and would have moaned deliriously had she not pressed her hand against my mouth.

At dawn she slipped from the room to the street. I had scrambled into clothes at the last minute. I looked a sight.

Standing on the steps outside was Metz, smoking a cigarette. The surprise of him at this hour blunted the moment.

'*Guten Morgen*.' He smiled, as facetiously as he dared, my scowl a patent threat to him.

I saw Elise to the street. She turned in the direction of the hospital. We parted with only a whispered promise of seeing each other as soon as possible.

There was only that evening. U-69 was scheduled to leave Lorient the next day.

I turned back and headed inside, glaring disgustingly at Metz as I passed. He shrugged his innocence.

The day had not started well, but there was no choice but for it to improve. There was a great deal more to be done in preparation for U-69 setting out to sea. The *Kriegsmarine* saw to it that thoughts of young women were set decisively aside.

I would do my best to pay absolute attention.

THE *ZAMALEK* IS A NIFTY VESSEL. SMALL ENOUGH TO manoeuver the perimeter of the convoy, yet with enough speed to maintain her regular position at the rear of the sixth column. Her reputation is solid, her successes a welcome boost to the morale of any convoy. Convoy ON 165 is the fortunate band of merchant vessels to have her in their midst.

Johnny Gilbert is one of fifty-five crewmen aboard, the closest he's come to being an enlisted man. He doesn't doubt the risks of the mission. He is as much in harm's way as any man serving the Royal Navy. Of course, he knows all too much about being in harm's way. Yet this is different. He feels himself in the brunt of the war, and relishes the thought of actually laying eyes on a U-boat for the first time.

The *Zamalek* is part of the Royal Fleet Auxiliary and flies the Blue Ensign. She's not an attack vessel, but she has guns to defend herself, including four 20mm Oerlikons, and a Bofors 40mm mounted aft, and the navy men aboard to run the show should they be needed. What the *Zamalek* is truly equipped to do is deal with the consequences of an attack, should one of the convoy's ships be savaged by a German torpedo.

Her captain, Owen Morris, is a gritty Welshman known, in his lighter moments ashore, to display an operatic tenor. Aboard ship, he is all business.

He has never failed her, and his ship has never failed him, through the worst of circumstances, whether it be heavy seas or relentless attack by enemy aircraft or the ship sense needed to pluck aboard those left stranded on the frigid ocean. Four months previous, after a particularly perilous outing as part of an Arctic convoy to Russia, Morris was awarded the Distinguished Service Order, only the second merchant navy man ever to receive it.

During the first week out, Johnny has been soaking up everything he can about the workings of the vessel. Captain Morris expects it of his men, even of a ship's assistant steward, but Johnny is not only out to impress the captain, or to repay him for taking him on. He's bound and determined to go at it man-to-man with the Germans.

He's being naïve, of course, and in the back of his mind he knows this. The chances of him actually encountering a German are next to nil. What he might see is the black outline of a U-boat, if he's lucky (or unlucky, as circumstances allow). Or a periscope slipping above the surface of the ocean, although there's very little chance of that either, given what a tough task it is even for the watch officers. In addition to the fact he hasn't been issued a pair of binoculars, and the sniper's scope belonging to his father went down with the *Caribou*.

Nevertheless, the unrealistic hope is there and it's what drives him day to day as the convoy plies its course across the Atlantic. The first part of their routing took them down the Firth of Clyde, with the island of Arran and then Ireland to starboard, before picking up more merchant ships out of Liverpool and finally penetrating the open ocean. The ships manoeuver through the swells to take up their stations in the sequence they've been ordered to maintain throughout the crossing. Close to forty vessels—British,

Norwegian, Yugoslavian, Danish, Swedish, Estonian, Hungarian, Greek, American, Icelandic—in eleven columns, 1000 yards between columns, 800 yards between ships. The convoy measures six nautical miles wide and 1.3 nautical miles long.

Commodore Casey is in charge, aboard the *Empire Mariner*. The man knows convoys, having commanded several since the war started, and he knows submarines, having served on one during the First War. He had been navigator aboard two destroyers and the Royal Navy had assigned him the intricate task of finding berths for the ships racing back from Dunkirk.

The *Empire Mariner* is at the head of the central sixth column, the same one assigned to the *Zamalek*, in the column's rear position. The two vessels will maintain regular communication and through the duration of the crossing will develop a unique bond. Captain Morris is a second pair of eyes for the commodore, in the event that a ship loses power and strays away from the pack, or is involved in some incident that deflects her off course. The two men know there are always incidents, mechanical or weather related. Their nerves are pitched and braced constantly for incidents of the other type.

The *Zamalek* was built in 1921 in Troon, on the Ayrshire coast, and twenty years later refashioned into a rescue ship in the shipyards of Govan, Glasgow. The refit was not without its deficiencies, considering the *Zamalek* was one of the first of the small cargo ships requisitioned by the British Admiralty. The biggest challenge was providing space to quarter those plucked from the ocean during any rescue, in addition to a sickbay and operating theatre.

Her first refit added two-berth cabins for twenty-six officer survivors and messdeck bunks for fifty-six ratings. It made for very cramped quarters, but, as it turned out, not cramped enough. On her tenth trip out the *Zamalek* jammed aboard 109 survivors. A second refit added more survivor berths. Then, a year later, came the infamous PQ 17 convoy to Russia. In heavy seas the *Zamalek* was relentlessly pounded by enemy aircraft but survived, having shot down one of them, eventually making it to shore in Archangel with a count of 154 survivors pulled from the Arctic waters.

It's what earned Morris his DSO, as Johnny heard from crewmen who had gone through the ordeal with him. They are immensely proud of their captain, and think of him as the only person who could have done it.

Rest assured, Johnny is in good hands.

His confidence is doubled by the fact that the rescue ship, like the *Empire Mariner*, is outfitted with HF/DF equipment. The *Zamalek* has aboard three crack radio officers just to handle the "Huff Duff" as everyone calls it. It pinpoints high frequency radio transmissions sent between U-boats and their headquarters. That, and the breaking of the Enigma code, has breathed new life into the convoys and their escorts. No longer are U-boats attacking with impunity. If they do turn up, the Royal Navy is ready and able for the bastards, one of radio officers tells Johnny. It brings a smile to them both.

Convoy ON 165 has been assigned Escort Group B6. A week into the crossing and Johnny sights the arrival of F-class HMS *Fame* and V-class HMS *Viscount*, a pair of Royal Navy destroyers, the escort's big guns. With the corvettes already attached to the convoy, B6 now delivers a battery of seven warships. It's led by forty-one-year-old Ralph Heathcote in the *Fame*.

Commander Heathcote has been in charge of the *Fame* since August. His first escort duties across the Atlantic came in October. The wolfpack *Wotan* sank eight of convoy SC 104's ships, with a loss of only two German U-boats, including U-353 at the hands of the *Fame*. In December the destroyer re-crossed the Atlantic. Partway out she was reassigned to ON 154 which had endured all-out assault by the eighteen U-boats of wolfpacks *Spitz* and *Ungestüm*. Heathcote was handed command of the escort after its senior officer collapsed in a state of nervous exhaustion. The man's inexperience had cost the convoy fourteen ships and 546 men, one of the greatest convoy disasters of the war.

Confidence in a safe passage is not running high. It never is. That is as expected, especially as Casey, Heathcote, and Morris witness the last of the RAF's Consolidated Liberators flying back to base in Iceland. The four-engine bomber had reached the limit of its reconnaissance range.

On February 15, the convoy enters the infamous Greenland Gap, a 300-mile stretch of the North Atlantic south of Greenland. To most navy men it is The Black Pit. At this point convoys lose aircraft cover until they near Newfoundland, where other RAF bombers will pick up where their counterparts in Iceland left off. The Black Pit is a sore point with the Navy. Its commanders believe it doesn't have to be so wide, that those in charge of aircraft assignment are giving priority to Bomber Command operations over Germany. More aircraft and a base in Greenland would save merchant ships and countless lives. Their argument continuously falls on deaf bureaucratic ears.

Johnny is getting the lowdown from Hugh MacKinnon, a Scot and his newfound friend aboard the *Zamalek*. Hugh is from Skye, a Hebridean, like so many more of the crew, men who know their way around boats, handpicked by Captain Morris for that reason.

Johnny has let it be known that his paternal grandfather came to Labrador from Scotland. He could have been from the Hebrides, Johnny tells Hugh, although he had never met the man.

Hugh is not a deckhand, nor one of the rescue crew. Like Johnny, he works in the galley. Yet if ever there is a need to help out in a rescue, they'll know what to be doing.

Hugh's accent took getting used to, and when the Scots get together it's still a hopeless tangle, but one-on-one he and Johnny manage fine enough. Over his years aboard the *Caribou* Johnny has lost some of his own accent but he can plunge back into it when he has the mind to. Sometimes, for the fun of it, they rant on, swopping expressions, vying to outdo each other, to the exasperation of their galley mates.

Hugh has something he takes particular pride in—his knowledge of whisky. Back on Skye he was assistant to the distiller for Talisker, before the war came calling. In any case the distillery closed a year later, its supply of barley needed to offset a shortage of food that had become steadily worse since the war began. Hugh has closely guarded two bottles, one for the trip outbound, the other for the return, filled from a small cask given him when he gave up his job. He is counting on the supply outlasting the war, and himself along with it.

The other shipmates have learned to ignore Hugh's single malt. He's not about to share it with anyone. That's why Johnny is left a bit dumbfounded when Hugh takes him aside one evening after clean-up from supper and offers him a dram. Wee though it is, Johnny is honoured and if there is any one thing that solidifies their relationship, this gesture is it. With the dram comes a lesson on how the whisky should be drunk, what Hugh calls taking in its full breadth. It's a ritual that sets them apart from the others aboard.

Johnny has always liked being removed from the general chorus of men. He's come to derive satisfaction from turning up in unfamiliar places, taking on the unknown, even in how the sinking of the *Caribou* has separated him, given him a reputation for survival. He's less concerned than most aboard about what the crossing might hold.

Hugh surely thinks it odd, that brashness coming from someone who never stepped aboard a rescue ship before. He warns Johnny not to get cocky, tells him he'd pay for it in the end. The captain doesn't appreciate overconfidence, especially from someone who hasn't earned it. Johnny sinks back a notch. At least on the surface, in the face he presents to his shipmates. He keeps it from them, his thirst for revenge, his conviction to get even for what the Hun did to the *Caribou*.

It overrides all his thoughts. When the others talk about their women he says nothing. When they tell him of how they'd spend their days on Islay or Lewis, he says nothing. Only to Hugh does he talk much, and it occurs to him it's like his father and Sam in the First War, how they had each other, the sniper and his spotter. A fellow only needs one good friend. The others get in the way.

One day Hugh puts it to the fellow. There's a lot inside him not getting out. He pushes and pushes more until Johnny can't handle it.

It's all a fuck-up. A fuck-up. He tells Hugh more than what he's told him already—Miss Fitzpatrick, the Strickland youngsters. He stops there. Hugh knows there's more. There's a girl mixed up in it somewhere.

The Jerries have had their way, he tells Johnny. The next few months will tell the tale. Either the British turn it around or they're fucked for good.

His bluntness stiffens Johnny. He's forced to stretch his mind around Hugh's cynicism. It knocks him back another notch.

On February 15, convoy ON 165 gives up its first ship. Johnny steals time on deck to witness the *Atlantic Sun*, the third ship in the column next to them, drift out of position. The vessel is an American tanker, empty except for water ballast. She had left Iceland and joined the convoy the week before. It was bound to happen, a ship forced to relinquish its position because of mechanical trouble. The tanker is left on her own. With luck her engineers will have the problem taken care of quickly and the *Atlantic Sun* will catch up and slip back into the fold. There is concern for the ship and its crew, but there's nothing more to be done.

At sea the assurance of a woman falls away. She waxes to the ephemeral, shaped by tenuous yearning. You dare not embrace anything as tangible as hope. You strain to set her aside. Your heart becomes a muscle.

My days and nights are dense with the strain of frigid seas growing perpetually rougher, fog encasing us like a thick, impenetrable blanket. All a constant foil for our plans. We vent our frustration at the "wretched weather" or some such words, terse addendums to the positioning reports to headquarters. A consequence of the herding tactic Dönitz has perfected. *Rudeltaktik*. Wolfpacks. I think we sound better in their language than our own.

They must smile at the limp record of *Haudegen*. For the remaining band of thirteen U-boats, and the seven more that have come and gone, we have nothing to show for our prowess but two merchant ships, one British, one Norwegian, 13,000 GRT. Such a damnable tally.

Most of the U-boats have breathed together for a month, now strung out in a half-circle northeast of Newfoundland, thirsting for a convoy, parked in their paths, by headquarters' calculations. Fuel and its companion, time, are running low. What will arrive first—a convoy or the call to re-cross the Atlantic to France?

There is always the negligible prospect of crossing paths with a convoy on the way back. Another of my cohorts from Dänholm,

Soden-Fraunhofen, did exactly that. The unfortunate, aristocratic prig.

It was him, in his U-624, who sank one of the two boats *Haudegen* can claim. He nailed a pair of torpedoes into a straggler just south of Greenland. A few days later, his fuel running low, he got the call he'd been waiting for. As his luck had it, on the way back to base he brushed up against another convoy.

Luck has its drawbacks. U-624 was on the surface, reporting back to headquarters, giving a British bomber enough time to pick up her transmission. The RAF mauled the U-boat with depth charges. All forty-five crewmen are never to be seen again. Soden-Fraunhofen always did have too much to say.

Regardless of the weather, *Haudegen* doesn't linger about the Gap with any certainty. Morale is doubly low. Two weeks ago our Dönitz, *Der Löwe,* announced he has relinquished tactical command of the U-boats. That he's been appointed commander-in-chief of the entire navy. He's moved from Paris to Berlin. I suspect there isn't a U-boat commander who was not disgruntled at the news. Word trickles down to the lowest ranks and the reaction is much the same. Dönitz imbued us with confidence in the worst of times.

We have been forty-five days at sea. Grinding routine and the cursed weather have stretched us limb from limb. Solid sleep is impossible unless we dive. We haven't had a stable meal for weeks. Tempers erupt, insults fly. My rant only quells the mood to something sufferable. A taut undercurrent of restlessness engulfs us all.

Finally, word from headquarters ordering *Haudegen* to disperse. Four boats which still have an adequate supply of fuel will remain and form into a new pack, *Taifun*. The luckless mob. The other nine of us are ordered back to base.

Gott sei Dank!

The unbridled cheer rings through the boat when I make the announcement. Some captains would reprimand their U-boatmen for such bravado at the thought of exiting the front lines. I am not such a captain. Every man has his limits and is deserving of relief. Myself included.

We have our route plotted and approved within the hour. U-69 has seen the last of its grudging inaction. We are on our own. That in itself is reason for optimism.

For the first time in weeks I dare let my mind linger on Elise. But only briefly.

Chief plunges in with a vengeance. He's calculated the surface speed that will eat up the least fuel, given that in a couple of days we should be out of these blasted seas. We'll make it back to Lorient with little fuel to spare, but we'll make it. We'll dive if we have to, but I'm thinking there'll be nothing to drive us under.

Then, not two hours out, Hebestreit calls me into the radio room with news of U-607, another *Haudegen* castoff on its way back to France. What is Mengersen up to now? One more of the glaringly bright lights of the *Kriegsmarine*. Likely a dozen boats to his credit. I can't think he'd have the good luck to add to his tally, when we're not even on the prowl.

Not so. A Yankee tanker. Another 10, 000 GRT he calculates. My unreserved envy goes out to him.

A lone fish, though it must have once been attached to a convoy. For sure Mengersen is scouting about for more, although with the weather growing more desperate by the minute, there'll be little chance of success. The Beaufort scale has reached wind force nine. We've launched ourselves into another North Atlantic storm.

I armour up for the bridge. The waterproofs—rubberized leather coat and trousers—are dead heavy and cumbersome.

Add to that a towel wrapped around the neck, fleece-lined gloves, sou'wester knotted under the chin.

Up the ladder, I listen for the sound of seas breaking over the hatch. I chance an exit when there's an interlude between them, lunging upwards and onto the bridge, pitching the hatch closed behind me.

It's hellish outside. Rain, as near to ice pellets as it gets, lashes sideways across the bridge and into the miserable foursome. The sky is stone grey, the clouds thick and hostile. The horizon gives way to black, roiling seas marked by dense streaks of foam. The wind roars, gusts so strong the watch have themselves harnessed to the railing, their garb utterly awash in seawater, only a narrow band of reddened face exposed.

'*Kapitänleutnant.* Sir.' Umbeck likes the fact I have made the effort to emerge from the bowels of the U-boat. The other three turn to me, their weather-ravaged faces hinting at pride in what they've endured.

I recount the story of U-607, but it's all so much shouting into the wind that its purpose is defeated. If we were to spot an enemy vessel, what U-boat captain would ever think of mounting an attack in these seas? None with any common sense. In fact, what concerns Umbeck is the fact I'm standing untethered with the U-boat lurching through the mountainous swell. He grabs me as a huge ridge of sea spray whips into us. I'm upended in a second, Umbeck still holding tight. He drags me to my feet. I latch both hands to the rail, knuckles swelling inside my gloves. I offer up a grin.

There's a second pummeling to ride out, before making the wisest choice—to head back down the tower, leaving the watch crew to do its job. The bridge Johnny is there, smiling, quick to help me out of my sopping clothes. I can't get rid of them fast enough.

'The North Atlantic is not what navy tailors had in mind,' he says.

I'm drenched to the skin, practically naked now, all the time braced against the ladder to keep upright. The fellow, eager to salvage my dignity, passes me a blanket. I throw it around me as best I can, then make a game move toward my quarters while he carts the clothes away, heading aft. He'll find a place for them on either side of the stern torpedo tube, the best place aboard for drying.

In these seas crewing a U-boat is damn sobering business. We all need relief. I track down Chief and order him to take us under. Schieder looks at me as if questioning my sanity.

He follows orders. Within seconds of the watch safely inside he starts the dive. At fifty meters there's equilibrium again in our world. A man can stand upright and not be praying his head doesn't get jarred against a hand wheel. A man can sit and eat tasteless stew from a plate that is not being slopped to the floor. There is pause enough to regain reasons for being aboard a U-boat. I work my way through the boat, talking to them man-to-man, fitting Lorient into the days ahead of us.

There is calmness that won't last, yet it's enough to reassure the men that in time there will be normality. Most of them set out to restore a scrap of decency to their routine, to clean up as best they can, reshape themselves into some semblance of the crewmen who boarded the ship seven weeks ago. It marks their optimism.

Only Hagemann would have us think he couldn't care less about his appearance. His beard is crusted with remnants of his last meal, the cut he sustained to his forehead where it smashed into the eyepiece of the periscope needs bandaging. He was too contrary to get it stitched and figures the seawater wash it gets when he's on watch duty is enough to keep away infection.

For hours on end he speaks when spoken to, but nothing otherwise. He would have been happy enough to stay on the surface, or he would have us believe that is the case.

'A little breathing room, *Oberleutant*.'

A grunt of sorts, close to an actual word, but not one. As if he would prefer to be ignored, though when he is he takes it as an affront.

I persist. 'You're an old sea dog, Hagemann, before your time. You're bound to get called up.' I've never been so direct with him. It's true, they are desperate for commanders. They'll have twenty-four year olds in their sights any day now.

It's the closest thing I've seen to satisfaction in a week. Hagemann is a strange bird at the best of times, but with his latest bout of petulance he's driving the rest of us crazy. The unfortunate three who have to share the bridge with him have the worst of it, and a few private words from me to disarm his behavior is not about to accomplish much.

It's the first watch officer's job to keep the torpedoes trim and ready for loading. It's never anything but a challenge, what with half the crew bunked next to them, but these past few days of bucking the storm it's been a madhouse and the word getting back to me is that Hagemann is being an unrestrained ass about it all. Of course he himself is too contrary ever to get seasick, so why the hell should anyone else? How can U-boatmen worth their salt collapse in their bunks in the middle of the day, vomit cans wedged between their bunks? There is no damn difference between day and night in a U-boat.

'No eels are going anywhere in this weather.'

'I'm doing my job.'

'And it's my job to keep us all sane.' He'll defy me more if I don't put a stop to it. 'A few days left to Lorient—your demands are not worth it, *Oberleutant!*' He's never seen much of a temper from me before.

He sulks away and the next time I see him he looks at me, something close to a nod. He's no tidier, no less sure of himself, but it stamps out the complaints, at least the ones getting back to me.

U-69 stays under as long as it takes for the men to get a solid few hours of sleep, enough to revive them before renewing the fight with the weather upstairs. I give Hebestreit orders for a half hour of the gramophone before the ascent. Nothing to break the mood. Beethoven, I tell Hebestreit. I let him decide exactly what. By now he knows what pleases me and what doesn't.

I'm about to leave my quarters and search out Chief when I stop and sit on the edge of the bed, working through the opening notes of the Moonlight Sonata, a favourite of my mother. They are notes to cut into a man if he were to remember how she wrapped me in her embrace when I first left home for training. She had her uncertainties, but she gave into me. I would hear of nothing else.

That one choice defined all others, and those others are defined by a man bending over a vast map of the North Atlantic. I came to think of myself as poised at the end of Dönitz's pencil, the one passed to *Kapitän zur See* Godt, passed with the power to pinpoint me where he wishes.

Me and a boatload of others. There's the stroke. To a man they're unreservedly my charge, Hagemann included, perhaps Hagemann most of all. I cannot make a step but they are in step with me. Not a misstep but they dutifully concur. I appreciate a Hagemann. A man needs his doubts, or where is there beauty in it?

Hagemann shines again, as I knew he would. We rise to the surface, into seas no less brutal. The men take them on with renewed alertness. Lorient looms ever closer.

Hagemann heads the first watch, and it is Hagemann's hawkeye, through the bruising rain and unrelenting swell, that catches what no one is expecting.

Ships heading east. They have to be part of a convoy.

I order Chief to alter course to fix on them. I'm on the bridge in minutes, one hand gripping the rail, the other trying to hold the binoculars stable enough to see in the direction Hagemann is jabbing his finger. Only the weather keeps his frenzy in check, tangible through the vice grip he has on my arm to keep me upright and steady.

'Do you see it, *Kapitänleutnant*?' My new rank jars past the frenzy of emotion.

'Yes. Yes.' It is blurred by the fog and rain, but there is no mistaking it. Two ships for certain, and scant indication of more.

One an oiler, likely to supply other ships, more proof of a convoy. The second is a speck, no more than 1500 GRT. Not worth a torpedo. Then it dawns on me—one of the ships the Tommies send along to pick up survivors. With any luck, it'll be put to good use.

And what do we make of it all? That is for the *Kapitän* Godt to decide.

'Latch on to them, Hagemann.'

Hagemann smells blood. I see it in his face. He can barely contain himself.

I fight my way below and out of the dripping gear. Hebestreit is waiting in the radio room. He looks up, his face pinched with tension. Pencil in hand, blank message sheet in front of him.

A brief sighting report, not another word. There can be no strike without direction from Paris. The chance we take. The enemy's new devices have smartened them up, but Dönitz has vowed they'll never crack the cipher machine.

Beta. Beta. Quadr AK *1541. Eastbound convoy. Course 225°.*

Hebestreit runs it through Enigma. Transmits it to Command.

The wait is agonizing. Chief stands close by, both of us gripping what we can to level ourselves. We both know an attack in this weather would be lunacy. Beyond that it is impossible to read him.

The odd crewman maneuvers past us on his way to the engine room, or back again, the stench of oil fumes trailing him. Stand in one place long enough you experience the air in its full glory—humid sweat, garbaged food, oil, diesel. In these seas the boat can't be properly vented and what you breathe is not much better than the concoction that passes for air when the boat is submerged.

The boat is taut with anticipation, crewmen pitched at the prospect of the almighty word.

What comes thrusts the boat into a frenzy.

'Alarm!' blares Hagemann down the tube, at the same time sounding the bell.

Chief is off like a bullet, shouting '*Auf Tiefe gehen!*' to drive us under. The sodden watch drops down the ladder, Hagemann bellowing still as he secures the hatch. 'We've been spotted! A fucking destroyer.'

In this fog, a last minute sighting. Chief will need to be quick as hell.

If anyone can, it's Schieder. The hydroplanes are already reset.

'Flood!' he orders. Water surges into the forward ballast tanks. The air vents seal shut, the diesels stop, the electric motors cut in. The bow pitches forward and beneath the waves. Men race forward for the extra weight. The flooding of the aft tanks is timed to perfection, and within minutes U-69 is under and levelling out.

Tentative relief, yet dread that the worst is yet to come. All ears are bent for the sound of depth charges. Breathing stops and only consciously restarts, until minutes pass and still nothing. We've escaped or the escort ships have other plans.

Gradually, uniform breathing returns. Minute by minute the tension dissipates, until there is consensus there'll be no attack.

The destroyer won't chance wasting depth charges. He thinks we're not going anywhere.

He's right. Only far enough to rise comfortably nearer the surface, to within range for picking up transmissions from Command. Godt will have made up his mind what we should be doing.

Hebestreit hands over the decoded message. *U-69 to shadow convoy. Transmit homing signal. Taifun join U-69. Returning Haudegen boats rejoin. Operate on convoy to the very limit of fuel supply. Refuel at sea. U-boat tanker U-460 near Azores. Coordinates to follow.*

U-69 is in the dead centre of this escapade. U-607 can't be far off, the others racing toward us, however they can in this weather. Godt's order from his immutable desk in Paris is for U-69 to stick doggedly to the convoy. The promise of attack glinting in his eye.

A U-boat captain complies, as eagerly as he knows how, unquestioningly. Hagemann even more so.

Chief will have none of it. 'We'll do damn all in these seas.'

'Give it time.'

'What bloody time?'

He is right. We have no time.

'The destroyer is picking up our signal. Is he not!' he yells in the direction of the radio room.

The enemy is the one with time.

Johnny has his routine to keep him straight.

Although *Zamalek* is neither, she is more a navy vessel than a merchant vessel. At least Captain Morris likes to think of her that way. He brings a military turn to life aboard the ship. Each day starts with inspection. The man is a keener for precision and cleanliness.

As he walks through the galley, the stewards lined up stiffly before him, he is looking for signs of unpreparedness. Food and its consumption are at the core of a well-run ship. Given the fact that at any time there might be a rescue operation and with it an influx of hungry bodies, some in desperate physical shape, he demands constant affirmation that nothing will go wrong.

The stewards are keen to comply, knowing that the captain's nod of approval and terse few words of validation are worth every effort they make. They appreciate the fact that he never raises petty issues, is not ferreting out trivial concerns, solely to assert authority. Just like their captain, every crewman has put his life on the line by signing up to return to the vessel. Captain Morris values loyalty above all else.

Johnny, being a new fellow in a collection of veterans, feels he has to make the extra effort beyond what the captain expects. His uniform is faultless at the start of each day, his shoes shine brighter than any others. His hands and fingernails have been scrubbed to a dull red, his face precisely shaven, with never a nick that a styptic stick doesn't hide. When he removes his hat it reveals closely cropped hair slicked tight to his head with a smear of Silvikrin hair tonic.

Hugh invariably smiles when he first lays eyes on Johnny each morning, knowing that, come their first rescue mission, he will be as dishevelled and dog-tired as the next fellow. Still, he sees in Johnny a decent confidence now, something that will stand him in good stead. It bolsters Hugh's ego—having done that for his mate, a best friend who's not a Scot.

Everything is set against the framework of the weather. It has grown steadily worse, battering the rescue ship with forty-foot seas, relentless wind and icy rain. Nobody goes on deck unless they have to, and there are times even the most daredevil of the deckhands won't risk it for fear of being toppled and swept overboard.

There is an upside, Johnny's been told. In these conditions, and with visibility so poor, no U-boat captain could mount an attack.

It's no consolation to Johnny. For days he's been picturing a U-boat looming alarmingly out of the fog. In his mind the weather had been adding to the menace rather than diminishing it. He resists the reality.

Like he did aboard the *Tudor Prince*, Johnny volunteers to service the bridge with canisters of hot tea and biscuits, no matter the time of day or night, needed or not. Generally the men are appreciative, and occasionally a watch officer will give him a quick look through his binoculars. It's something.

With the pounding the *Zamalek* is taking, attention on the bridge is fixed on keeping the ship in its designated position, like it is in the bridge of every ship in the convoy. Except for the captains and watch officers in the lead ship and the escort vessels, no one has much mind for U-boats.

Then, without warning, comes an urgent transmission from Commodore Casey—*HF/DF confirmation of U-boat 049 degs 00' North, 043 degs 30' West within 75 miles.* Captain Morris can hardly believe what the radioman passes to him. Where there's one there's likely more.

He alerts the crew, though it goes without saying that the weather is playing in the convoy's favour. U-boat captains are not fools, as much as a wolfpack might be licking its lips at the thought of sending more ships to the bottom. On top of that, intelligence coming down the line confirms that the U-boats have been on patrol for so long they must be desperately short of fuel.

Morris is relieved to be punishing through the weather. In another couple of days they'll be nearing Newfoundland and under RCAF cover. In the meantime he's satisfied the escort destroyers have everything in hand. In recent months their HF/DF equipment has proven itself several times over. Morris assures his crew that no U-boat will get within striking distance without being detected.

The crew face the weather with renewed energy. They can feel Newfoundland in the near distance.

Somewhat reluctantly, Johnny comes to accept the situation. The U-boats he now imagines lurking about are too far away to be any threat. Hugh is happy enough about it all, despite being tossed about at every turn, and so should Johnny.

There's always the next trip.

Seize the lead. Muster the u-boats. Forge ahead. Outwit the convoy. Attack.

The deal is simple. Its execution not so. The homing signal is gold through their headphones. No more the stealthy wolf. The enemy has my scent.

It is hellish to fix a position in this fog. Transmissions from Command are butchered by atmospheric interference. Nothing more than damn noise and crackles.

Leave it to pragmatism and to instinct.

Schieder and Hagemann are at each other's throat. Hagemann takes it as disloyalty to be questioning Command.

'What, Chief? Are you thinking we clutch our fucking torpedoes like a dog with a bone?'

Schieder refuses to be cowed.

'Your shot is likely to improve in this weather, is it, Exec? You are suddenly the mastermind of the foul-weather slaughter?'

'Straighten yourself. The seas are making you weak-kneed.'

'Damn you.'

'Fool.'

It's been brewing for days. Tension seething to implode. I let them at each other.

Then put a flat-out stop to it. Glaring in their faces, beneath my breath, 'Damn you both.'

They look at me but not each other. Stupefied, bizarrely subdued.

For the moment they wander off. Leaving me with my decisions.

FOR HOURS OUR U-69 HAS BEEN THE FACE OF U-BOATS IN the North Atlantic. U-69—the history-maker. The very first VIIC U-boat commissioned by the *Kriegsmarine*. November 1940, commanded by the imperturbable Jost Metzler. 60,000 GRT. Proud wearer of the Knight's Cross—as we U-boat captains like to say, something to cure an itchy neck. And a fucking hard act to follow.

Yet the man had a sense of humour, a formidable trait in a U-boat captain. It was under Metzler that U-69 became "The Laughing Cow." Its emblem painted on the conning tower, *La vache qui rit*, is that of a cow on a French cheese box. Command had given orders for a snorting bull, like the rest of the flotilla. But the officer Metzler left in charge couldn't come up with an image and settled on what he found on a cheese crate lid lying about the docks in Lorient.

Metzler was amused, and when the officers at Command headquarters chuckled in their own imperious way, he chuckled too. As did we all when we first laid eyes on the cow. *La vache qui rit*—a French dairy cow laughing recklessly on the conning tower of a U-boat. How un-Teutonic.

I never met Metzler. His presence looms large about this ship; half the men who served with him are still aboard. By all accounts a notable captain. There is no need to amplify the applause.

You know a captain by his numbers and the futile race to catch up now that the Happy Time is long past. The convoy is a distinct temptation, though by all reasoning an imprudent one.

Reason plays but a part. Orders play a stronger one. Command delights in master plans, laid out an ocean away. Godt knows U-boats, at least U-25 which he commanded for eighteen months. And I will add, prior to the war.

'He's experienced nothing of the North Atlantic in February.'

Hebestreit is my sounding board. I expect him to agree, but he is hesitant to take sides. He retreats to his headphones, trying to decipher anything at all through the static.

'Are we alone then, Hebestreit?' He looks at me, but says nothing. I know we are, or he would have already confirmed otherwise. 'Shall we go at it alone?' I mutter with some enthusiasm, knowing it goes unheard.

The answer of course will be all mine, not his.

All the time he transmits our intermittent homing signal, as Command has ordered. All the time it must gladden the heart of the convoy. Their radiomen, without doubt, shine with pride at what their instruments can do.

The cynic is having his way. I stand with Nietzsche. The Nietzsche before he went mad. *No price is too high to pay for the privilege of owning yourself.* My studies with Lachnit served me well. What colour would Marc paint these seas? An uncompromising red? A steadfast blue?

It is Umbeck who interrupts my good sense and brings me back to the deed at hand. Umbeck is looking queerly unperturbed by the upset of the last few hours. His face features the beard which for weeks he has been urging to something other than a downy embarrassment. For what point it serves, he trims it regularly, unlike most aboard who let them have their way, at least to the time we are in sight of our homeport. His uniform, too, is in better shape than most, bereft of the concoction of stains accumulated by other officers.

If he is to impress me, he has succeeded, for what it matters. More than anything, his façade stands in contrast to the slovenly Hagemann.

I am getting a bearing on Umbeck. He is out to set himself apart. Which serves his sanity I assume. We all have our ways. I am not about to fault him at this point. I don't have the energy.

'All is well, *Herr Kaleu*?' he says.

'Well, *Leutnant* Umbeck? Yes. A matter of time.'

'For the others to catch up?'

'Yes, to catch up. That is a good way of putting it.'

'Then we attack,' he says, as a matter of course, though with no nerve. He is no doubt aware of the opinions flaring between those higher in rank than himself.

'Imprudent in this weather?' I say.

It is not for him to agree or disagree. He has not been aboard U-boats long enough to have a mind of his own.

'The attack would be at periscope depth?'

Umbeck barely has my patience. In less grinding times I would remember that I, too, was once a naive watch officer. Before I witnessed the sounds of the *Bismarck* descending to her grave. That sobered me.

'Waiting on Command?'

'Waiting.'

The transmission coming through at that moment is not from Command. Hebestreit hands the copy to me as if it were a lifeline to a floundering man. From Rosenberg, confirming the position of U-201 within a few kilometers of us.

At last, an ally to share the burden.

Rosenberg of Crew 36, his time at Dänholm a year later than my own. His assignment to U-201, the Snowman, as it is nicknamed. Another VIIC, a few months after my assignment to the Laughing Cow.

Rosenberg, too, followed in the footsteps of the Knight's Cross, that of the glaringly successful "Adi" Schnee. Only Schnee's Knight's Cross came with Oak Leaves. His neck itched more than most. As did that of the *Schneemann* on his conning tower, a snowman painted with its own Knight's Cross.

Rosenberg with three ships to his credit, GRT not far off my own. An ally made to measure.

There's no choice but transmit directly to him. Likely the convoy has us in its sights already, so what more is there to lose.

I nod to Hebestreit. He'll keep it as short as possible. With prodigious luck, it will escape the convoy's notice.

Umbeck has been silent through it all. He stares blankly at me, thinking I might share Rosenberg's message with him. Instead, I send him in search of Hagemann and Schieder. He doesn't have far to go, not in a U-boat, not with everyone aboard tense as hell in anticipation.

Hagemann and Schieder keep what distance they can from each other, which is very little. Umbeck has stationed himself between them, an appreciated gesture.

'We have our comrade.'

'One?'

'U-201. Günther Rosenberg.'

They all know of Schnee and his U-201. They likely know men who served on her. Rosenberg is a different story.

'The same *Schneemann*, a new captain.'

No one says anything, stiffly silent until Umbeck interjects. 'As my grandfather often said, second thoughts are the best.'

We could do without the choice words. Exactly what he means by reciting them, I doubt if Umbeck knows himself.

Hagemann looks at him scornfully, feigning an effort to hold back. 'Let's see him sink six ships in a single patrol.'

No one needs to be thinking of that.

All three are awaiting my response. If not wise words, at least practical ones that would attempt the job expected of us, then allow an escape, both U-69 and our dignity intact. A tall fucking order.

I am smiling, which confounds them all, even Umbeck who has never known such a circumstance as this. If truth were practical, neither have any of us known it. Not until our periscope breaks the surface and what we have to deal with is erratically framed by its crosshairs.

Even lying in his bunk, the constant lurch and drop through the swell allowing him only broken sleep, Johnny rarely thinks of home. His mother and Sam, at a distance from the war, are safe enough.

His work keeps him busy, although no one aboard is eating much. Even the iron-gutted would have trouble keeping down a full meal. Few of the crewmen would ever admit to being seasick, but on this trip they are being severely tested. They suffer through their duties as best they can, are there when needed, but when they're not they weather the seas in their bunks. Once what passes for the evening meal is over, the galley cleaned and secured as best it can be against the heave of the boat, Johnny and Hugh do the same.

'Times like this I think about Morag.'

Johnny can't figure it. Their whole world battling gravity, their stomachs constantly threatening upheaval, and Hugh has his girl from Skye on his mind?

'She'll wait.'

'Will she, Johnny? I'm counting on everything being the same when I get back. It might be a right mess. A right fuck-up.'

Johnny depends on the fellow not turning morose, depends on their alliance to keep his own thoughts of women at bay. He lies in the bunk and tightens himself into a knot, thinking there's less of him to bang about, less in his mind to deal with, less to drive out.

Suddenly none of that matters. Captain Morris is on the horn, sending Johnny to his feet. He stumbles about.

Without fanfare Morris announces the escorts are breaking formation. In pursuit of the enemy.

Johnny rushes into oilskins, and for all he's worth to the open deck. He gets a grip on a railing, latching onto what the seas have offered up.

On orders from Command I set a course with u-201, launching forward for a closer look. No transmissions until one of us has something to offer. But for the steady whirr of the E-motors, all is silence.

Breath by breath, u-69 draws closer to the convoy.

Chief, eyes fixed to the manometer, monitors the speed and the gradual ascent to periscope depth, unwaveringly keen in his precision.

We all are standing in the control room, each man mutely questioning what comes next. No one wants to be the first to speak. As we near the surface, the boat begins to rock. We grip what pipes we can to stay upright.

I offer them, 'Patience, gentlemen. All together, patience.'

No impulse to rouse them with false bravado, no willingness to champion hope where we advance guardedly.

'Periscope depth.' The words discharged by Chief with equally quiet precision, ahead of him turning to us.

I'm already at the periscope, locked to the eyepiece, a hand gripping one handle, an arm hanging over the opposite one. The view clear of the fomenting sea, the sweep of the surface begins.

'Alarm!'

Dear Christ.

'Alarm!'

JOHNNY'S EYES LATCH ONTO THE DESTROYER. THE WAR-horse whose hunger for U-boats far outstrips his own.

Fame ploughs the surface in pursuit of something. Johnny strains his eyes ahead of the ship. The seas are too rough to discern anything but spray and foam. He strains harder but the lashing from the wind and icy rain forces his head away. He recovers before attempting to fix again on the seas ahead of the ship. It is impossible.

Suddenly there's an eruption in front of the destroyer, sending a huge plume of seawater skyward.

A depth charge.

Then another. Another.

There is one conclusion. A U-boat. The thrill of it charges through the Newfoundlander.

Explosions slap the U-boat like a sledgehammer. Tremors jolt the floor plates, driving our feet from under us. And us in heaps about the control room but for our brutal grip on the hatch ladder and the pipes overhead.

Damn you all! Piercing curses penetrate the ship, joined by the seething roar of the sea rushing to fill the vacuum left by the detonations.

All the time Chief is driving the U-boat under. He bellows at the man in charge of the hydroplanes. 'Hard down!'

The E-motors fire. Men from the engine room lunge forward, crouching headfirst along the control-room floor, through the officers' quarters, finally worming past the circular opening into the bow compartment.

Another goddamn blast rocks the boat, and another.

The destroyer is hurling whatever she's got on top of us.

Another blast and the lights go black.

'Auxiliary power!' The words are hardly out of my mouth when the lights flash back on.

'Damage report!'

Through the voice pipes rattle a string of responses. None reporting damage.

The ashcans have exploded outside the lethal zone.

U-boats have escaped worse. Though the worse is likely yet to come.

Suddenly there is a dreaded splay of pings, like pebbles striking a tin bucket. The soundman confirms it. 'ASDIC!' Needlessly.

There's not a man aboard who doesn't flinch at the sound. The destroyer is on to us. What might have been luck before has surged to certainty. More depth charges.

'A matter of time, gentlemen.' If the others are surprised by the force of my calmness, they shouldn't be.

I hold my grip, reminding them that the success rate of depth charges is a paltry five percent. That countless U-boats have survived a pummelling worse than what we are enduring. That Metzler and U-69 spent three hours under attack by dozens of ashcans and came out unscarred.

Chief, eyes latched to the manometer, reports we have levelled out at 150 meters. He looks at me, questioning if we should go deeper.

It's damn unlikely the enemy can manage any accuracy at this depth. Or with the sea conditions what they are on the surface.

'They might scare the hell out of us, but there's little fucking chance they'll do any more than that. Isn't that right, Chief?'

Slammed again by another pair of explosions! Steel plates grind savagely, then moan their way back to silence.

I regain my stance. The others can detect sangfroid if they look for it. Even when the silence is broken by the soundman's report of the destroyer's propeller. His eyes fix on me.

Steady. Schieder knows to keep our bow pointed at the enemy ship. To sit broadside would give the ASDIC signal more surface to strike. He knows too if we've sunk below a thermal layer, that would be something else to fuck the ASDIC.

He looks at me. In his mind are the hours we've been running underwater, how long before we'll have to surface and recharge our batteries. The more we move about the more we drain them.

Once more the rattle of pings! The destroyer has latched on again. It knows exactly where we're lying.

'Let the bastards try!' Hagemann yells. Up to now he's been pathetically quiet. His blood-strained eyes turn upward. 'Drop them, you fuckers!'

The game is on. Destroyer and U-boat, each one determined as hell to outfox the other.

'Hard a-starboard!'

Chief reacts with lightning speed. U-69 veers sharply, out of the path of the ashcans according to my guesswork.

Not this time. Not one or two, but a mad torrent of explosions! They tear our bodies limb by limb, jolt us about like marionettes.

The destroyer set itself directly on top of us. Flung charges from all sides of the ship and let them sink with more precision than we ever thought possible. Pelted U-69 with a grid pattern of ten or more. The navigator lost count.

We've lost common sense. Finally recover enough to argue whether to dive deeper and shake off the ASDIC.

Chief's fist is fixed atop the manometer. Another hundred meters and we reach our crush depth.

'VIIC's have gone a lot deeper,' I tell them. And survived to tell their stories.

I know what Chief is thinking. The same as what I'm thinking. The depth charges are not what they were in Metzler's time. They're heavier. They sink faster. Fewer seconds from when the soundman hears them hit the water.

And how much has the pounding we endured weakened us? Are there cracks and flanges ready to burst? How many fucking more will it take to do us in?

It's me who'll make the decision. I look from face to face around the control room. From Schieder to Hagemann. To Umbeck, to Hebestreit. To the trio of men who had been set for watch duty before we dove under. I stop at Wimmer. His face is wet with tears, and yet he smiles. He is thinking of his mother in Bremen.

We'll stay where we are. We'll chance it.

Cut our speed. Run silent, run steady. Give their hydrophones a run for their fucking money. Rid ourselves of all needless noise. No bilge pumps, no mechanical clatter. The word passes through the U-boat. Voices pale to mute. Movement to inertia.

U-69 shrinks to unrelenting secrecy.

Commander Heathcote rides out the grim North Atlantic in pursuit of the U-boat, mindful of the increasing distance between his destroyer and the convoy. His first duty is to the ships he's been assigned to protect, yet he knows ON 165 won't be making much headway, given the weather. He sees no need to halt the chase. At his back is the havoc the Jerries unleashed on SC 104 and ON 154. His hunger for revenge takes hold, grips him fiercely.

To add to the drama, he has a companion in the hunt. Lieutenant Commander Waterhouse in HMS *Viscount* has spotted another U-boat. The sub crash-dived and the second destroyer is in pursuit. Both Heathcote and Waterhouse are desperately keen to pummel the two U-boats with as many depth charges as they can drop with a measure of accuracy. This is the first chance they've had to use the stockpiles aboard, and they are chafing to put them to the test before ON 165 nears the end of its Atlantic crossing. Newfoundland is only 500 nautical miles away.

Destroyers are built for speed and maneuverability, and both Heathcote and Waterhouse are confident veterans at handling their vessels. Although they're well aware of the dismal success rate of depth charges, the new, improved ASDIC have given them strong readings on the U-boats. The wind and heavy seas are an additional challenge, but they're up for it. With only two subs in the vicinity they're determined to get the both of them, the bastards.

Johnny watches *Fame* lunge through the seas, indifferent to the waves pounding it broadside. The *Zamalek* has lingered behind the convoy. Captain Morris knows that if she's needed it will be in the aftermath of enemy action.

It's a rough ride, but Johnny is determined to hang in for as long as the destroyers have the scent of the U-boats. Heavy spray lashes over him, but it's nothing he won't withstand. He's as fit as he's been since escaping with his life from the *Caribou*. That memory is not lost on him. The prospect of an eye for an eye is embedded in his mind, and he knows he's as close to vengeance as he's likely to get.

His head is covered with a rubberized sou'wester. Frigid seawater has channelled a way past his waterproofs and soaked him to the skin. He's not about to give into it. Not with the round of depth charges he witnesses.

Seawater erupts skyward in a swirl of explosions encircling the *Fame*. It fires Johnny's blood. He's forgotten the cold. It's a brilliant spectacle, nothing he ever could have imagined. Whatever he's put himself through to get to this point has been worth it.

Retribution. The rightness of the moment rifles through him, and with another round of depth charges, played against the frenzied Atlantic, the fellow is euphoric.

It only takes one depth charge. Just one within that six-meter gap between immunity and mutilation.

When it comes we know instantly this is the one. The jolt wrecks our equilibrium, slapping us to the floor plates. We pick ourselves up amid a squall of voices from the officers' quarters.

'Pressure hull breached!'

I rush forward with an ungainly, broken gait, past the sound and radio men and to a clump of terrified officers.

'Where?' I shout at them. 'Where?' I expect a water leak but hear or see nothing. Neither there nor in the bow compartment beyond them.

'Smell it, *Kapitänleutnant*!'

I stare at the floor hatch. Unbolted, it would be direct access to the battery compartment below. *Oberfunkmatt* Sachse is coughing.

There is no mistaking it. The pungent odour of chlorine gas.

Perhaps no more than a minute crack in the pressure hull. Impossible to reach for repair. A projectile of saltwater rifled into the compartment, reacting with the battery electrolyte. Chlorine gas is invading us, poisoning our scant supply of oxygen.

Bearable for the moment, but it can only get worse. Coughing. Chest pain. Vomiting. Choking death within a half hour.

'Surface!' I shout back to Schieder. 'Now!' The only choice. And like hell, before the chlorine strangles us. While we still have chance to vent the U-boat and save ourselves.

Chief barks instructions to the hydroplane operator. He himself blows the ballast tanks, compressed air hissing through valves to drive out the water. Immediately the boat starts to rise. No one questions me. The chlorine gas has infiltrated the control room.

I get word to every man aboard, my voice through the speaking pipes slow and measured, betraying the anxiety crawling beneath my skin. What hell awaits us when the U-boat breaks into the open ocean?

The airtight doors between compartments are quietly opened and swung wide, joining the crew from bow to stern. The chlorine gas circulates throughout every chink and crevice of living space, lowering its concentration where it first escaped. We are all part of it.

Coughing can be heard from one end of the U-boat to the other. Above it, Chief marks the steady rise with anxious, but controlled precision, knowing well the dangers of ascending too fast. 'One hundred meters.'

Hagemann barks orders to his watch crew, defiantly loud, as if he wants to be heard in the seas above. Umbeck insists he be part of it. He forces Wimmer out of the way, snatching the fellow's weatherproofs for himself.

'Seventy-five.'

The coughing has become a morbid chorus. Some resort to their Draeger breathing apparatus and its bottled oxygen, meant to be used to escape a sinking boat, but now with the desperate hope of clearing their lungs.

Wimmer is dumbstruck at having lost his rightful place on watch duty. He ingests a mouthful of air and hacks himself into a corner.

'Shut the hell up!' Hagemann snarls, triggering a fit of coughing himself.

Finally, 'Fifty.'

'Quiet,' I growl. The control room turns dumb except for the throat lurch of suppressed coughing. 'Gentlemen, we heard it as children. Fear makes the wolf bigger than he is.' My gaze passes over each of them. 'Have we not?'

'Yes, *Kapitänleutnant*.' Only Schieder manages it.

It remains silent enough that the soundman's pronouncement, when it comes, as it must, is redundant. Through the coughing we can all make out the parade of pings from the enemy's ASDIC.

'*Leutnant* Umbeck, give him back his weatherproofs. Get your own.' I turn to Wimmer, 'Thank the second watch officer and get on with it.'

Their compliance is a distraction. But inevitably it comes.

'Twenty-five.'

I lead the way up the ladder to the conning tower.

But make no move to the periscope. We will break the surface, regardless. What greets us I will see unmistakably with my two eyes.

Six men stand at the base of the ladder, geared for the final ascent to the bridge, as fearless as our fractured wisdom allows. A clump of seamen, allies, compatriots, dogs for the Fatherland.

There is a vague image through a train window of a young cadet peering at the countryside, of a girl gracefully raising her hand. A knowing smile, rife with promise. She is my innocent. My unspoiled passage into manhood.

Our world has come to this, men clenched in imminent fate.

Raw conviction is set rigidly into Hagemann's face. It has beaten him to silence. It is there in Ehrlich and Langhof, if tempered by short, unruly breaths. Umbeck has willed himself to stoicism. There is nothing he won't be willing to square himself against. Only in Wimmer is there emotion. He struggles desperately against it, holding his breath and stiffening his jaw as if that might be enough to dry his eyes. Coughing comes as a relief to him.

Our binoculars are our salvation. They hang against our chests with impunity. Their heft is the heft of weapons. We grip them like godsends.

Our ears are set to the chief engineer. More seconds pass, unheralded.

'Stand by,' Chief announces from the control room below.

I pull myself onto the lowest rungs and lurch upward. To within reach of the hatch. I tackle its wheel with mindless fervor, unlocking the hatch abruptly. I throw it open.

Saltwater streams through the opening. Chased by a surge of frigid fresh air. In our wake, the control room swells with crewmen inhaling deeply, gasping relief.

U-69 has barely broken the surface. The six of us scramble out in an erratic chain, onto the bridge, sodden faces into the turmoil. We fix on tethering ourselves to the railing, only then willing to confront the seas that pitch and surge everywhere around us.

The foul weather has not abated. It thrashes the U-boat, whipping spray over the bridge, morbid repetition of what we knew before. Each of us with one hand bound to the railing, the other fiercely pressing binoculars to our eyes. Three hundred and sixty degrees portioned by six.

There is a moment of relief, of squinting through water-smudged lenses past mist and fog and seeing nothing. None of us with a scrap of anything to report. While the U-boat rigorously vents the foul air inside it. The gods have tentatively sapped the dread that engulfed us all.

Wimmer, the youngest, the man with the most years to lose, touches my shoulder.

'Herr Kaleu.'

I turn and his blurred eyes set into mine. His Zeiss hangs at his chest. He leans to one side for me to have my look.

I know better. I know not to acknowledge the gesture. I know to breathe the icy, untainted air to the limit of my lungs. To mock the moment.

When it comes into focus, its outline is brutal. Turned against the elements, forging toward us.

For a second, instinct is scorned. I defy the urge to spurn the inevitable.

Until, 'Alarm!'

Frantically untethered, we crowd the open hatch. Graceless men plunge one after another into the congested tower below.

I hold out to the last.

My final sight, their final salvo—the raging bow of the destroyer set dead in front of us.

I haul shut the cover, twist the wheel and hang by it into the open air.

With the mad anticipation of more depth charges about to peak, he can just detect it through the turbid curtain of spray, yes, the rise of a conning tower through the water, yes, the unshrouding of a grey, iron tube in a trough of the waves.

Before he has chance to emit a futile cry into the wind-brayed seas, Johnny's eyes fix on *Fame*'s slow, deliberate sweep in the direction of the U-boat. The destroyer's bow aligns with the sub broadside, and like a feral sycophant the ship powers forward. Johnny suspects there might even be Germans on the bridge above the conning tower. He hopes to hell there are.

The 1,400 GRT destroyer bears down on the U-boat. Although the Royal Navy discourages ramming because of the risk of damage to the attacking destroyer, *Fame* crushes the U-boat's port quarter, crumpling the outer hull. Heathcote is confident the onslaught was enough to penetrate the 20mm-thick steel of the pressure hull. He is triumphant.

Johnny watches the tortured sub succumb to the waves. It slips beneath the surface, stern first. The sea washes over the tip of its periscope and the German U-boat is gone. Johnny lets out a cry of approval. He glories in the triumph.

Of course he has no idea which of the many German U-boats it is, just as he had no idea which U-boat it was that sank the *Caribou*. It's no matter. Justice has been dealt. Johnny will hold relentlessly to this moment as long as he is alive.

THE IMPACT JOLTS ME FREE. I PLUMMET TO THE CONNING tower floor.

Asunder. Stunned. As every man aboard. A clump of bodies grope about to right themselves. Lunging forward, careening back. Heaved up and under.

The U-boat's list batters its symmetry. Batters us squarely against a snarl of gauges and hand wheels, the shaft of a flashlight twitching about the black.

Ice-raw seawater sloshes up from the control room, coils about us. Churns through tangled limbs.

The struggle keeps two of us above water, the other four below, bashed and frozen senseless.

The fight that survives in me tears at my sluggish clothes. Rids me of what I can.

The rising water slows. At chest level it confronts the pocket of cornered air. We two struggle to survive, our feet piled on those who didn't.

A death watch. A fraternal death watch.

The air compresses as the boat sinks meter by meter.

My mind locks into breathing. Nothing more, nothing unmarked by doom.

'Herr Kaleu.'

The pressure against my ears makes it an agonizing lament. Wimmer, the poor bastard, gropes for me through the black.

His sodden weight hangs on me. I ram him clear. He has nowhere to go.

'Herr Kaleu.'

The water rises more. He flails about to keep his head clear.

'Goddamn the water,' he sputters.

I stand on a dead watch officer and rack my neck backwards.

My eardrums explode.

Goddamn the war.

She swirls about the waters, her hand outstretched, a smile to fill a soul. He stands, his arms wrapping out the chill, barely out of reach. A man returned. A man dying to revolve the world around her. To remake it. To remake it everlasting. Though she cannot abide by him. She cannot. She drifts away. He stands immovable, weighted under. A man transfixed, his heart crushed.

FEBRUARY 1945

One will be for Buzz. Another for Charlotte's friend, whose name he can't recall.

Hank's training and promotion to first lieutenant put him inside the Plexiglas nose cone of a B-17 Flying Fortress. Fort the crews call their bombers, just as Mickey is what they call the H2X radar that will lead them to where they'll drop their bombs. The Fort that Hank has been assigned to, like all the other B-17s, has its own name. Delicious Dame it's called and the dame is painted on the bomber just behind the cone, a reclining pin-up blonde in a two-piece polka-dot swim suit and high heels.

At 0800 this February morning, 1400 bombers of the American Eighth Air Force will leave their bases scattered across southern England. Like the rest of his airplane's nine-man crew, Hank is out of his bunk at the Podington barracks by 0430, ready for a full gas-load mission. The last of the RAF Lancasters are just touching down, back from the nighttime bombing of their target city, the same one the B-17s are due to strike in a few hours.

Breakfast is substantial. Real eggs, canned bacon and Spam, and thick, black coffee. A half-hour later the crews are trucked through the cold and dark and into raw light outside steel huts. Inside, Hank discovers who will be with him aboard his B-17. Some men he's flown missions with before, some not. The crews are always changing. Inside the hut a large map is pinned in place, black tape tracing the mission's route. After a few patriotic preliminaries from the CO, the briefing officer reveals their target.

Dresden. Hank has never heard of it.

He listens intently. He always does. Hank's the bombardier. The payload (sixty percent 500-pounders, forty percent incendiaries) is in his hands. Dropping bombs is the only reason he and eight other airmen are about to fly deep into German territory. If anything goes awry one or more of them could end up dead from attack by German fighters or ground flak, or they could be forced to evacuate, drop under parachute into enemy territory and be dragged off to POW camps.

The briefing officer predicts negligible flak defense. That's good. It's a lot better than his last bomb drop over Berlin. That Fort limped back to Podington, part of its tail shot off, the tail gunner one damn lucky G.I.

The number is up to a half-dozen now—men Hank trained with who haven't made it back. He works hard not to think about it, though he's not always successful. He can't afford to have it in his head if he's going to get through and see Texas again.

The flight altitude is announced, together with the time schedule. Watches are synchronized.

Bombardiers and navigators have a further briefing, to detail their targets and the weather conditions they are likely to encounter. Some squadrons are assigned the train marshalling yards on the western fringe of the city. Others, including Hank's lot, would target the city's centre. If there is cloud cover they'll put Mickey to use.

Trucks take them to the equipment room where they outfit themselves. At an altitude of 25,000 feet the temperature inside the bomber will fall to minus fifty degrees Fahrenheit. Hank will need his multiple wool layers and electric Bugs Bunny flying suit. The Air Corps supply a survival kit in case he's shot down. He gives up anything that might identify him or his mission, all except his dog tags, the same ones he kissed after making it aboard the lifeboat in the Cabot Strait.

Another G.I. truck transports him to the hardstand where the Dame awaits her crew. There's a thorough run-through of the equipment, in the wake of the ground crew's final check. The pilot and co-pilot have their instrument test list. The gunners load their ammunition. Hank and the navigator assure themselves their Norden bombsight is in top working order.

The ground crew supply them with a last cup of coffee. The pilot and his crew await word for the start-up of each of the four engines. It promises to be a long day, but Hank is as ready as he will ever be. It is in this interval that he thinks of home. He thinks of an end to the war. He thinks of being back at base and the time between missions when he and his buddies will have a night out in an English countryside village, and where he's sure he'll be seeing Sarah once again.

Four hundred and sixty-one B-17s head to Dresden. They fly in units of three squadrons, a total of twenty Forts, in standard box formation. The route takes them across the North Sea to the Dutch coast. The skies are clear and there is hope they will remain that way. The Forts have dozens of P-51 fighter escorts to protect them. While not in the lead squadron, neither is Hank's B-17 in the low squadron in the low group, the first target for German attack planes, what the flyers call the Purple Heart Corner.

As the Forts roar up the Elbe, the Plexiglas cone encasing Hank gives him and the navigator the perfect panoramic view. Hank's eyes sweep the landscape in anticipation of the bend in the river that marks the city. Just like the briefing predicted, there's only minor flak. He must fix his mind on the lead plane and ignore whatever might be popping against his aircraft. In any case the B-17 is a warhorse and good for it.

If the visibility holds it will be the ideal scenario, but cloud cover gradually solidifies and there is no choice but revert to Mickey. Hank has only to keep his hand on the lever and his eyes on the lead squadron to know when to make the drop.

Although he has no visual sighting of the city there is no doubt the B-17s are approaching Dresden. Through the cloud cover rise columns of black smoke. The city is burning from the RAF raids the night before.

Hank concentrates all the harder. At this moment he is essentially the one flying the airplane, for it is his call to fly straight and level and directly in the direction of the target. Just after twelve noon, as the aircraft plough through the columns of smoke, he sees bombs being dropped ahead of him. He pulls the lever that opens the bomb bay and releases the two racks of bombs that make up his payload.

In ten minutes, 771 tons of hellfire descend from the skies over Dresden.

Hank knows no more about Dresden than he did from the start. He sees nothing of the devastation the bombs and incendiaries inflict. He's just happy his B-17 is turning around and heading back to England. If all goes well, they will have landed by late afternoon, ready for debriefing and just in time for supper, another bomb run behind him. It's been a good day, one of his easier missions, and there's reason for cautious optimism. There's talk the war could be over before the year is out.

ACKNOWLEDGMENTS

Land Beyond the Sea was researched and written over several years, with parts of it first coming to public view as a stage play. My writing efforts were supported by many people and groups, and to these I am especially grateful: Anne and our family, a constant source of strength; James Langer, editor, who worked beyond measure for the good of the book; Breakwater Books and Westwood Creative Artists, caring professionals all; Donna Butt and Rising Tide Theatre, for their production of *Lead Me Home*; Mike Westcott, for his translation of portions of the U-boat log; Rona Rangsch, for pursuing the genealogical records in Germany; and Arts NL and the Access Copyright Foundation, for their financial support.

Historical fiction relies on the workings of an informed imagination. Its creative direction is underpinned by individual records of personal experience and the weight of academic research. The following sources are exceptional: the personal narratives of *Caribou* survivors Gerald Bastow, Alex Bateman, Aloysius Burke, Jack Dominie, Thomas Fleming, Jack Hatcher, William Lundrigan, Thomas Pearcey, Gladys Shiers, William Strickland,

and Howard Yorke; the accounts of the tragedy by writers Douglas How, Malcolm MacLeod, and H. Thornhill; and the Magisterial Enquiry into the deaths of victims brought ashore in Port aux Basques.

Exceptional, too, are the biographies, autobiographies, and chronicles of U-boat captains and crewmen Lothar-Günther Buchheim, Peter Cremer, Hans Goebeler, Werner Henke, Werner Hirschmann, Wolfgang Lüth, Jost Metzler, Teddy Suhren, Erich Topp, and Herbert A. Werner, and the classic novel and film *Das Boot*.

Many thanks go to the Deutsches U-Boot Museum, Cuxhaven-Altenbruch, for the patrol log of U-69; Deutsche Dienststelle (WASt), Berlin, for the military record of Ulrich Gräf; the National Archives, UK, for its records of Atlantic convoys; and the Museum of Science and Industry, Chicago, for an extensive tour of U-505.

I am indebted to the U-boat scholarship of Clay Blair, Luc Braeuer, Bernard Edwards, Nathan M. Greenfield, Michael Hadley, Malcolm Llewellyn-Jones, Timothy P. Mulligan, Jurgen Rohwer, Eric C. Rust, David Syrett, Jordon Vause, David Westwood, and Kenneth Wynn; the accounts of St. John's during WWII by John Cardoulis, Steven High, and Darrin McGrath; the convoy rescue-ship writings of Arnold Hague, Murdo Morrison, Neil McNaughton, and David Wherrett; and the accounts of the USAAF in Europe and its bombing of Dresden, by Sebastian Cox, Marshall De Bruhl, and Kevin Wilson.

And many thanks are due the websites and the volunteers who contribute to them: uboat.net, uboataces.com, uboatarchive.net, uboatwaffe.net, warsailors.com, and wikipedia.org.